THE SECRET OF DR. KILDARE

THE SECRET OF DR. KILDARE

Max Brand™

Chivers Press
Bath, Avon, England

G.K. Hall & Co.
Thorndike, Maine USA

This Large Print edition is published by Chivers Press, England, and by G.K. Hall & Co., USA.

Published in 1997 in the U.K. by arrangement with the author's estate.

Published in 1996 in the U.S. by arrangement with Golden West Literary Agency.

U.K. Hardcover ISBN 0–7451–4942–1 (Chivers Large Print)
U.K. Softcover ISBN 0–7451–4953–7 (Camden Large Print)
U.S. Softcover ISBN 0–7838–1846–7 (Nightingale Collection Edition)

The text of this Large Print edition is unabridged.
Other aspects of the book may vary from the original edition.

Set in 16 pt. New Times Roman.

Printed in Great Britain on acid-free paper.

British Library Cataloguing in Publication Data available

Library of Congress Cataloging-in-Publication Data

Brand, Max, 1892–1944.
The secret of Dr. Kildare / by Max Brand.
p. cm.
ISBN 0–7838–1846–7 (lg. print : sc)
1. Kildare, Doctor (Fictitious character)—Fiction. 2. Physicians—United States—Fiction. 3. Large type books. I. Title.
[PS3511.A87S33 1996]
813′.52—dc20 96–20903

CHAPTER ONE

The patients who came from the ends of the earth to consult Dr Leonard Gillespie, had been drawn to him by his fame as a miracle-worker or sent by baffled physicians of every country. Now, for three days, they had been brought by old Conover, the Negro who presided over the waiting room, not into the stormy presence of the great man, but to the young intern, James Kildare. He was neither very big nor very noisy and as a rule he failed to impress the people who had been drawn by a famous name; only a small minority saw in him that penetrating flash, that swiftly working instinct which seems almost foreknowledge and is characteristic of the born diagnostician. Kildare, accepting the great post almost guiltily, like a thief on a throne, nevertheless worked three days before he was completely stumped. Many a time when he had reached the end of his own trail of knowledge, he looked up in despair at the closely printed tomes which filled the walls of Gillespie's library, and as he stared, some page flickered in his memory, or the voice of Gillespie came back to hint at the clue of the mystery. So for three days he had not been guilty of a single gross error while the continued stream of feet came in over the blurred pattern of the rug where tens of thousands had stood before them. Instinct helped him through many a pinch. The great Gillespie himself used to say: 'The mind comprises nine-tenths of our being, and therefore a doctor who isn't part faith-healer is no damned good. A doctor who lacks human understanding is like a coal miner without a lamp on his hat or a pick in his hand.' Beyond a natural gift and the teaching of Gillespie, that human understanding helped Kildare through the first three days. Gillespie, in the meantime, was giving himself up to the work on his laboratory experiment. On the fourth day Kildare at last reached his impasse.

He sat with the laboratory reports in his hand, sweating a little as he stared at the boy, but what he really saw was the mother in the background. The lad was twelve, neatly turned out from the shine of his shoes to the gloves in his hand. In spite of his worn, sallow face there was still a fire in him, gradually dying. When his courage failed, he would fail also. In comparison the mother was like a kitchen slavey sent out with the young master. Rain had shrunk her cheap jacket until the sleeves were inches above the wrists and the bottom of it flared out before it reached her hips. She had a round, common face. The pain she had endured gave her the only distinction. Long-continued trouble had thumbed in shadowy lines and hollows of anxiety. The silence of Kildare as he stared at her boy frightened her to the heart, but she tried to wheedle the bad moment away.

'It's God's mercy that we've got *big* hospitals, doctor,' she said. 'Young or old, there ain't a chance that you could go wrong on a case with all them wheels turning and turning to set you right; not when you got a whole army to lend you a hand.'

Kildare tasted the bitter truth for a moment in his throat before he spoke it.

'I'm afraid that I can't help you,' he said.

Something stirred, like a whisper of wind, in the corner of the room behind him. That would be Mary Lamont. She was an excellent nurse and steady as a clock in emergencies, but the hopeless cases broke her down. He could feel her now like an extra burden on his mind. Then something struck the floor with a soft shock. Mrs Casey had dropped her handbag. The boy, stooping quickly, picked it up. He touched her with his hand.

'Steady, dear!' he said, and his concern for himself was so much less than his trouble for her that the heart of Kildare gave a great stroke of pain. Mrs Casey had created a masterpiece that was now about to be stolen from her and from the world.

'He can't help me! He can't help me!' she said over and over two or three times, looking into the future and finding it a black emptiness.

The boy put an arm around her and turned apologetically toward Kildare.

'Shall we go now, sir?' he asked.

'Yes,' said Kildare crisply.

Mary Lamont opened the exit door. She tried to make herself professionally matter-of-fact, but her voice was wobbly as she murmured: 'This way, please.' A girl as young as that was no good for this work, he decided. He liked having her around. She freshened the day, and she had a bedrock, honest faith in him that gave Kildare strength, but he would have to ask Gillespie for an older nurse.

'Thank you, Doctor Kildare,' the boy was saying as he went out.

'Wait a minute,' commanded Kildare.

They turned back suddenly. It was still the woman who seemed to stand under the death sentence, not the boy. Mary Lamont watched her doctor with a foolish brightness of expectancy. He scowled at the three of them.

'The other doctors—you mean that they're right?' Mrs Casey was asking.

'No. I think they're not right,' said Kildare. He watched the hope spring up in their faces. 'But I don't know where they're wrong.' They were struck blank again. 'Will you ask Doctor Gillespie if he'll make a special exception and see this patient?' he added to the nurse.

She blessed him with her eyes and her smile as she hurried across the room, but when she came to the door of the great internist's inner office, she hesitated a moment to gather her courage before she went in. Kildare could hear the pleasant murmur of her voice, not the words; then came the roar of Gillespie, hoarse as the barking of a sea-lion.

'I've told him before and I tell him again: I'll see *no*body! There's one last thing I can give medicine, and I've got it now in the tips of my fingers. It's almost in my hand if I'm let alone to work at it. What do I care about one patient, when I'm thinking of the lives of ten thousand? Get out!'

'Mother, let's go now. You heard him,' said the boy.

'Hush yourself, Michael,' said Mrs Casey. 'We'll go when we're sent. Wait for the word!'

Her fierce eyes dwelt upon Kildare as Mary Lamont came back into the room with her head bent so that they might not see the tears in her eyes.

'Doctor Gillespie finds himself too occupied,' she reported.

Kildare sighed, shrugged his shoulders, and crossed the room in his turn. 'I'll speak to him . . .' he said.

The inner office was stacked with cages of white mice that looked like filing cabinets, each with a white label and a glittering little water-tube. The odor of small animal life in the cages tainted the air as a drop of slime taints drinking water. The diagnostician, who had turned his private sanctum into a menagerie, had two of the cages on the arms of his wheel chair. In triumph he laughed aloud to Kildare: 'We're getting it, Jimmy! It's almost here! Look at this, will you?'

Six little white mice lay dead in one cage; in the other five were full of scamper and haste and only one was lifeless.

'Change the dosage a little and I think we've got it,' said Gillespie. 'There's the six of the control as dead as pins; and here's five out of six that the injections saved. Five out of six! What d'you think of it?'

'I want to talk to you . . .' began Kildare.

'I don't want chatter from you. I want work!' declared Gillespie. 'If you'll talk mice and meningitis, all right. Otherwise I have no time. We're going to whip meningitis into a corner, young Doctor Kildare. We're going to make it afraid to show its face. D'you hear me? We might even wangle a mangy little bit of a half-baked reputation for *you* out of this experiment. What are you hanging your head about now?'

His savage impatience made him jerk back his head. Brittle old muscles which failed to cushion the shock allowed a violent tremor to run down through his body. Kildare winced at the sight of it.

'I want you to see a patient. I want five minutes of your time,' said Kildare.

Old Gillespie banged the top of a mouse cage with the flat of his hand, and the mice began to weave a white pattern on the floor of the cage as they raced around it in terror.

'You don't want my time; you want my brain!' he shouted. 'And you can't have it!'

'He's a twelve-year-old boy,' said Kildare steadily.

'I don't give a damn if he's the prince of Siam or the emperor of Cochin-China!' cried Gillespie. 'I won't see him.'

'His mother's a washwoman,' said Kildare.

'Let her keep to her tubs and her suds then.'

'And she's making the boy a gentleman.'

'We don't want gentlemen; we want hard men who can take a chisel edge.'

'They call it pernicious anemia—the other doctors—and they're wrong.'

'I don't give a damn about anemia and other doctors and their errors; a lot of ignorant fools. I'm going on with this experiment and nothing else. You hear me?...'

'They call it anemia, and they're wrong,' repeated Kildare.

'What do *you* think it is?'

'I don't know. Here's the case history and the laboratory reports.'

'I'm not interested,' said Gillespie, snatching the papers. 'I'll have nothing to do with it ... Why don't you think it's anemia?'

'The blood picture showed no macrocytes,' said Kildare.

'Then why the devil are you wasting my time?' demanded Gillespie. 'Why don't you get him in here where I can lay eyes and hands on him?'

Kildare hurried back to the other room. With a handkerchief he rubbed the wet from his forehead as he beckoned to the boy. 'Doctor Gillespie *will* see you,' he said. This new accession of hope was too much for Mrs Casey. She sank into a chair and stared at the floor. Mary Lamont hurried toward her as Kildare ushered the boy into the presence of Gillespie, who was glowering at the laboratory reports.

Without lifting his head he snapped: 'Palpable spleen, Doctor Kildare?'

'Yes, sir,' said Kildare.

'Make a fragility test?'

'No, sir.'

'Why not?'

'The fragility test isn't one of the regular routine.'

'That's one of the damnations of the world—routine, routine, routine. People want to live by instinct, not by brains. Is the human race going to become a lot of damned insects? Use the mind more and routine less. Have a fragility test made at once.'

'Yes, sir,' said Kildare.

'Young man,' continued the internist, lifting his head and gathering the shag of his brows together, 'do you ever have pains here—up on your left side?'

'Yes, sir,' said the boy.

'You didn't tell me that,' said Kildare.

'I only have them now and then,' declared

young Casey.

'When you have those pains, your skin is turning yellow, eh?' asked Gillespie.

'Yes, sir,' agreed the boy.

'It's the dilating spleen,' stated Gillespie. 'I think this boy has haemolytic icterus, Jimmy. Have them get the spleen out of him and he'll be as fit as a fiddle again.' He pointed a sudden finger at the Casey boy. 'You hear me? You're going to be as right as a trivet inside of two weeks. Get out of my sight and tell your mother the news ... Stay here, Jimmy!'

'Thank you, sir ... thank you, Doctor Kildare,' the boy was saying as he left the room. He hurried his thanks in his eagerness to bring the great news to his mother; Kildare closed the door slowly after him.

'Are you going to break your fool heart because you missed one case in two hundred?' asked Gillespie, already at work on some Petri dishes that contained a reddish agar.

'No, sir,' said Kildare.

'You are, though. Or why do you stand there with that dumb look on your face like a wet hen?'

Kildare looked from the white hair of Gillespie, as wild as a windstorm, to the purple-blue beneath his wrinkled eyes. 'I'll never learn half what you know,' he said. 'I'll get used to seeing that. But what I see right now is that you're burning yourself up with this experiment.'

'That's a lie and a loud one,' answered Gillespie, dragging a loop of wire over the agar and commencing to transfer the colony of bacteria to three other dishes. 'I never felt better in my life.'

'Why does your hand shake then?' asked Kildare.

'None of your damned business. Leave me alone . . . till I need you, Jimmy. Will you?'

'Yes, sir,' answered Kildare, and went unwillingly from the room.

CHAPTER TWO

Hours later, and every hour like the weighty length of a day, Kildare was saying: 'Next, please!' when Mary Lamont answered: 'That's the end of the line for today.'

He shook his head at her impatiently. 'There are twenty more people out there!' he declared.

'I've sent them away,' she said.

'*You* sent them away?' exclaimed Kildare.

'I had orders from Doctor Gillespie.'

'But a Gillespie day never stops—it's from noon to noon,' protested Kildare.

'He won't let you keep those hours,' said the girl. 'He gave me express orders that the line is not to keep pressing in at you day and night.'

Kildare dropped into a chair, unbuttoned his white jacket at the throat, and wiped away perspiration from around his eyes. Hospitals are always too hot. He merely said: 'I suppose he's right. He's always right. I'd be a fool to try to imitate him. He goes in seven-league boots, and I'm only a measuring worm . . . I suppose he wants me in the laboratory.'

'No. You're to take some time off,' said Mary Lamont, watching his face. It was a familiar page to her now.

'Time off?' he repeated. 'That's right. Light work for the young horse. I'm damned tired of being young, aren't you?'

She turned hastily to pick up a fallen report and hide her smile. Kildare was plucking off the long white coat in which he worked. He always managed to get it as wrinkled and stained as a butcher's apron before the day's end.

'Little Michael Casey would be happy if you'd drop in to see him,' she suggested. 'The operation was perfect; and he's already two-thirds well. He's asking for you.'

'Tell him to save his wind; or let him thank Gillespie. But I'm glad he's doing well. Give them hope, and they're all giants. You notice that? Perhaps Gillespie will give him a word.'

'He wouldn't know how to talk to Doctor Gillespie; but they all know how to talk to you,' she pointed out. 'No matter how rough you are, they don't mind.' She waited for an answer, curiously.

'I'm one of them, and they know it,' he said.

'But they're out of the slums, and you're out of the country.'

'I'm born poor, and I'll die poor. They see that, and it's what matters.'

'Some day you may be a consultant at a thousand dollars a case,' she suggested.

'May I?' He smiled at this impossible future.

'Well, anyway, money can't buy the big things. It can't buy happiness and things like that.'

'It can keep them all in damned bright repair, though.'

'You're feeling down.'

'Haven't I reasons for being down?'

'Of course you haven't. There's not a man—there's hardly a man in the *world* who has your chance.'

'Good!' said Kildare, smiling wearily at her. 'Go on and be all lighted up. It's easy on my eyes.'

'You're not really unhappy. You're only blue. And that will go away like a cold in the head. What could you complain of?'

'Being broke—I'm tired of it. I'm sick of it. The kind of sickness that can't be cured except by a good third act—and I'm not able even to ask a girl to go to a show with me. Money? I'd like to bed myself down in the long green.'

'That's simply not true.'

'Don't act like a mother-in-law. Try to believe what I'm saying. I get twenty dollars a month. That's sixty-seven cents a day. If I go to

Sullivan's Saloon and buy two or three beers, a pack of cigarettes, and a sandwich, I've burned up my whole income. Wait a minute.'

Under the troubled eyes of the nurse he took out a shallow handful of silver and of dollar bills.

'Here's six bucks and a half. Mary, will you go to a show with me tonight?'

'No. You see me every day. You need somebody new.'

'I don't want your advice. I want *you*. Come along, will you?'

'Of course I will. I'd love it.'

'That's right. Pretend a little. Nine-tenths of any party is the pretending that goes into it.'

'Jimmy, don't be difficult. I really *want* to go.'

'You know what you're being?'

'What?'

'Bighearted,' he said, and walked away from her. Over his shoulder he called: 'See you in a half hour?'

She had not moved from the spot where he left her. She was looking after him with worried eyes and forgot to answer his last question.

When he got to his room, he found Tom Collins stretched out on one of the iron beds. He was so thin that he looked like a vacant suit of clothes with a head and hands stuck in the apertures.

'How about a beer at Mike's?' asked Collins.

'No.'

'How about two beers at Mike's?'

'I'm taking a girl to a show.'

'You're what? What sort of a girl?' asked Collins.

'One that likes to relax; that's why she puts up with me. Nobody tries, and so nobody gets tired.'

'Maybe you've got something—for an internist,' said Collins. 'Look out for that box on the floor…'

But he had given the warning too late and Kildare caught his shoe on the rough edge of a flat packing box that projected from beneath his bed. The old leather tore like paper. The whole toe of the right shoe was left in tatters. Kildare, looking solemnly down, wriggled his stockinged toes.

'Is that your only pair of shoes?' asked Collins.

'It is,' said Kildare, 'and there goes my party for this evening.'

'Don't be a dope,' said Collins. 'I've got more cash here than I can use, and…'

'Quit it, Tom,' said Kildare. 'But who brought this damned box?'

'Old Creighton, the carpenter. He said that he couldn't pay you in cash so he brought you that.'

Kildare tore off the top layer of composition board, lifted the paper packing, and exposed a small model of the Rockefeller Center, done with a cabinet-maker's most delicate miniature touch.

'A waste of time,' said Collins.

'Of course,' answered Kildare. 'But that's why my family will like it.'

Heavy tape was holding his shoe together when he went down to Mary Lamont with the big, flat box under his arm. She looked like somebody's sister, not the probation nurse who had been working with him. It was the first time he had seen her out of uniform, and she took his breath. She had on a wine-colored coat of a material as soft as camel's-hair, and a hat to match with a quill of yellow and orange stuck in a brim that furled up or down by surprise. Also she wore a scarf the color of sunlight.

'You're too expensive,' said Kildare. 'I couldn't take you even on trial. Put yourself back on the shelf, Mary . . . I mean, seriously: Look what's happened to my shoes, and now the only show I can take you to is a secondhand shop.'

She refused to stay behind in the hospital, however. The best of any party was simply to get out in the open, she said. So she walked over with him to the express office, where he sent off the model to his mother in Dartford. Then they were in a cellar store buying for two dollars and eighty-five cents a pair of half-soled shoes that once had cost ten or twelve.

'Now what?' he asked.

'Why can't we just talk?'

'We'll pick up a beer in Sullivan's Saloon then,' suggested Kildare. But when he had her there in the back room he was worried. There were three mugs talking loudly at a corner table, and for the first time in all his hours at the old saloon, he noticed the sawdust on the floor.

'Is it all right for you to be in this sort of a place?' he asked.

'Of course it's all right,' she said. 'Men like to talk in dark corners.'

'There's no giggle and jitter about you,' said Kildare. 'That's one of the ways you're different . . . What'll you drink?'

'Beer,' said Mary Lamont.

'You don't want beer. I can be a little more expensive than that.'

'I want beer,' she insisted, 'if it's on draught.'

'I'm going to hate the blighter who marries you and takes you away,' said Kildare. 'Hello, Mike. Two beers when you get a chance.'

'Okay,' said Mike. He went over to the corner table and said grimly: 'Why don't you guys pipe down and give the doc a chance to hear himself think?'

'What doc?' one of them asked.

'It's Kildare.' said Mike. 'Don't you know nothing?'

'Is that him? I thought he'd be twice that size. Let's take these into the bar . . .'

They went out. 'Hi, doc. How's things?' they said.

'Stay where you are,' urged Kildare.

'Ah-h-h, we know when a guy wants elbow room,' said one of them, and winked at the intern. This remark tickled them all, and they went into the bar on a great blast of laughter.

Mike came back with two wet glasses of beer.

'You shouldn't have troubled those fellows,' said Kildare.

'Yeah, and why not?' asked Mike. 'Why shouldn't you have your beer in peace, like usual?'

He was rubbing off the table with a painful thoroughness, throwing side glances at the girl.

'We used to see a lot more of you, doc,' he complained. 'But maybe you got better things to do with your time.'

'No, Mike. But I'm standing double duty now in the hospital.'

'He doesn't like me,' said the girl as Mike left the room. 'He thinks I'm a bad influence.'

'Mike? He likes everyone,' said Kildare.

Big Weyman, the ambulance driver, entered the room and lounged back toward the table of Kildare.

'Mind if I ask you something, doc?' he was saying.

'It's all right,' broke in Mary Lamont. 'It's only I, Weyman.'

The ambulance driver stopped short.

'Yeah, what d'you think of that dumb Mike telling me the doc was in here with a—Excuse me, Miss Lamont.' Weyman went out in haste.

'Was he trying to take care of me?' asked Kildare.

'Did Mike send for that gorilla of a Weyman because he thought...'

He sat up straight in his chair and looked angrily at nothing in particular.

'People are always going to try to take care of you,' stated Mary Lamont.

'Do you mind telling me why?' he asked politely.

'Because you get absorbed in things and forget about yourself. Bulldog, bulldog ... you're always finding a lost cause and locking your teeth on it. That's why I'm picking on you, Jimmy. I want to find out what hurt you so much today.'

'Gillespie,' said Kildare. 'Can't you see that he's burning his life out and pouring himself away working day and night on this meningitis experiment?'

'Do you mean that he's in *danger*?' she asked.

'Of course he is. Every old man is suffering from an incurable disease—I mean old age itself is a disease. There's my own father out there in the country in need of a sort of help that I can give him; but he's only an ordinary man. A Gillespie—why, every month or day that's whittled away from his life is a gift that's gone from the world.'

'Is that what upset you?'

'Isn't it enough? I've got to find a way to make Gillespie slow up. How can I do it?'

'I don't know,' said the girl, 'but I'm sure that you'll find a way, regardless of expense.'

'Why do you smile when you say that?' asked Kildare.

'Because you're always getting ready to spend the last breath in your body on something or other.'

He sat back to consider this strange statement and fell into such a brown study over it that before he knew it both their glasses were empty.

CHAPTER THREE

Martha Kildare wangled it so that Beatrice Raymond came over to see the box opened when Stephen Kildare brought it home before lunch. Mrs Kildare knew that Jimmy and Beatrice, without the slightest malice on either side, had turned their lives away from one another, and she was perfectly convinced that eventually she would be able to arrange a match between them; in the meantime she did what she could to keep them fresh in one another's memory. Jimmy's note read: 'Dear Mother, I'm passing on to you a present given to me by a patient who knows that interns can't take money. Maybe you have room for it somewhere. Anyway, there are things like this in town, so why don't you come to look at them and let me see you at the same time?' That was all the note said.

'You see,' said the mother, 'he doesn't write letters. He doesn't know *how* to write letters.'

Beatrice Raymond smiled at her. She said: 'You don't have to explain him, Aunt Martha. You don't have to apologize either. I was reading in a book about young men the other day, and now I know all about them.'

'Do you?' asked Martha Kildare, watching the smile of the girl.

'Yes. The book says that they're only half real.'

'What's the other half composed of then?'

'Legend,' said Beatrice.

'But what legend, my dear?'

'The legend of what they want to be or think they are.'

'Did you read that or discover it for yourself?'

'I may have dreamed it,' confessed Beatrice Raymond.

'And what do young girls do about them—supposing the girls care a rap?'

'Young girls are made up of equal parts of patience, stupidity, and hope, aren't they?' asked Beatrice Raymond.

'Well, that's what the poets used to say about them.'

'Was it ever true?'

'No, thank God . . . Look, Beatrice!'

She had worked off the cover from the box and the model sparkled under their eyes.

'Stephen!' called the doctor's wife. 'Oh, Stephen! Come here!'

She hurried into the front room which had once been changed from a New England parlor sanctum into an office for young James Kildare before the old people knew how far away ambition was driving their son. Once altered, they never had been able to bring it back to the old semblance. They could not take down the diplomas from the wall or displace the big mahogany desk, and yet every memento of Jimmy gave them a sadder assurance that he never would come back to them again. They had glimpses from time to time, but his devotion was like that of a novice to some great and ascetic religious order. They felt about him equal parts of pride and grief.

Old Doctor Kildare was found by his wife studying a letter which he crunched almost guiltily in his hand and then tossed into the fire. It glanced back from an iron firedog and rolled out onto the hearth again.

'Come see what Jimmy has sent me,' she called to him, but when he came hurrying out she lingered for a moment to pick up that soiled and crumpled letter from the floor; but she did not open it until her husband had left the house to answer a patient's call. Then she took Beatrice Raymond into her confidence and smoothed the typewritten sheet of paper face down on the table.

'There's something in this that hurt the doctor,' she said, 'and he's trying to hide it from me. Beatrice, do you think it's wrong for me to look into it?'

'If I were you I wouldn't dare,' said Beatrice. 'But then, I'm not you.'

Attacked in this unexpected manner by conscience, Mrs Kildare looked down to the floor and tried to find a ready way out.

'There was such a look about him, Beatrice,' she explained. '*You* take a glance at it, dear, and tell me if there's anything I need to know about poor Steve.'

'We'll look together,' said Beatrice. 'That'll give him two people to blame.' She turned the letter face up.

'It's from Doctor Carboys!' whispered Mrs Kildare. 'What has Steven been doing with that terrible man.'

'But isn't Doctor Carboys a very fine physician?'

'He's one of those good men who never have anything but bad news . . . I can't make it out. You read it aloud, Beatrice.'

So she read: 'Dear Steve, I have the complete laboratory reports now on the blood, urine, and nonprotein nitrogen. These are all within normal limits, I'm very glad to say. The electrocardiogram and the X-ray plate of the chest are not quite so favorable, however. I am sending them over to your office tomorrow.

'I have to consider your symptoms after eating, of a marked sense of fullness in the upper abdomen together with enduring substernal pain, some constriction about the chest, radiating pains down the inner side of the left arm, shortness of breath and an impending sense of death. In addition, as you know, in recent years you have had signs of renal changes, your heart has become somewhat enlarged to the left, and you become more and more easily fatigued.

'In considering these things, I must remember that you are not growing any younger, and I've tried to take that into consideration, but these are the findings on the heart.

'The ECG report is as follows:

'Auricular rate 78
Ventricular rate 78
Rhythm regular
Voltage variable

'QRS excursion greatest in lead 1, upright in lead 1, diphasic in lead 2 and inverted in lead 3. Slight slurring is present. Lead 4 had a relatively small Q. PR interval is .20 seconds. T is upright in leads 1 and 2. ST interval is slightly above the base line in leads 1 and 2.

'The slurring and variable voltage indicates the presence of some myocardial damage, and this, in conjunction with the raised ST interval in leads 1 and 2 and in lead 4, the relatively small Q, probably indicates the presence of coronary changes. The inversion of the QRS couples in leads 2 and 3 indicates the presence of left axis deviation.

'In addition the chest plate shows, together with the enlargement of the heart to the left, elongation of the aortic arch with possible sclerotic plaques visible along the arch of the aorta.

'Now that I've given you the facts, you can interpret them yourself clearly enough. You hardly need to have me say in black and white that I believe you have had a coronary occlusion. You ought to go to bed and stay there for a long time. Bed rest for two or three months is my idea for you, and this should be followed by a complete change of occupation to remove all stress and strain. My dear Steve, it is a terribly unpleasant duty for me to say that you may live ten seconds or ten years, but the chances for the ten years are not so good. Tell me when I may come to see you, and we'll talk over all the details.

'Affectionately yours,

ARTHUR CARBOYS.'

* * *

The scientific terminology had kept Beatrice stumbling until she came to the last paragraph, but this was expressed in such layman's language that its meaning was all too clear; her voice lowered as she proceeded with the reading. The thousand wrinkles of pain in the face of Mrs Kildare made her look down, and she did not look up at once after reaching the signature, and she still was trying to draw words into her mind when she heard the steady, firm voice of Mrs Kildare saying: 'I suppose it's the end.'

'What will you do?' asked Beatrice pitifully.

'Everyone manages to get along somehow. If we can't run, we can walk. If we can't walk, we can creep. If we can't creep, we can lie in bed and remember better days. But Jimmy must not know. Not a breath of it must come to him, or he'd throw up his career and come home to help.'

'But what else is it right for him to do?' cried Beatrice Raymond. 'You can't let him stay on in the city...'

'Why not?' asked the mother fiercely. 'We've tried to help him forward. Are we going to hinder him now simply because we've lived too long? I'd rather we both dropped dead—now—this instant!'

CHAPTER FOUR

The head of the hospital, Dr Walter Carew, had only two facial expressions—one weary and one ferocious. This evening he looked merely weary as he regarded Kildare across the shimmer of his great desk. He kept his chin on his fist and his face inclined, which exaggerated the likeness between him and Cicero; it was a trick which he had used for so many years that he was unconscious of it now.

'How often have you been here on the carpet, Kildare?' he asked. 'I mean, how often has your medical career faced a firing squad in this office?'

'Twice, sir,' said Kildare.

'Twice—twice—' nodded Carew. 'It seems more often than that. Most of our young men get out of the hospital before I have a chance to know them, and I suppose they can thank God for it; but I've had occasion to know *you*, my friend.'

This speech suggested no ready answer, so Kildare was silent. Carew went on with his reflections. 'A hospital is like a family of children, a preposterous, huge, sprawling, bawling family of brats, always out at the toe and the elbow, always with empty bellies, winter coming on and no coal in the cellar. For twenty-five years I've been growing more and more tired of dodging and stealing and fencing and fending for this damned institution. It's enough of a public hospital to make it subject to every twopenny politician in the town; and it's enough of a private hospital to send it begging to every rich man's table in hope of scraping together a few crumbs of charity. As sure as my name is Walter Carew, I've been a beggar. I wear my trousers out at the knee. If I'd said as many prayers for the good of my soul as I have for the sake of this place, I'd be too good for the earth; I'd be in heaven already.'

He lifted his head and looked upon Kildare more wearily than ever. 'Directly or indirectly, you've been a source of benefactions or a cause that has attracted them to this hospital directly or indirectly.' He was repeating himself like an after-dinner speaker. Now, however, as he came to the point, he faltered a little. 'Do you think I can steal you away from Gillespie for an evening, my lad?'

'Doctor Gillespie is in the middle of an experiment...'

'The meningitis affair. I know. I know.'

'He seems to need me for one thing or another most of the time.'

'I know that too. He sharpens the claws of his ugly nature on you; he wipes the boots of his bad temper on you. That's his greatest need of you, isn't it?'

Kildare, looking back through his memories

of the storms which recently had been blowing about his devoted head, smiled a little.

'He seems to find me useful—in one way or another,' he said.

Carew stared at him, open-mouthed.

'And you don't mind him?' he asked.

'No, sir. Not a bit,' said Kildare.

'I wish I could say that,' sighed Carew. 'For twenty-five years that great bully has harried me up and down and back and forth like an old rag of paper in a high wind. I'm the scapegoat of this hospital, not the head of it. Within its four walls everything good is attributed to Leonard Gillespie, and Walter Carew is damned day and night for everything that goes wrong. Admit that that is true!'

'No, sir,' said Kildare. 'I don't think so.'

'Don't try to flatter me,' sighed Carew. 'There's not a suture that breaks except through my fault; if an ambulance tire goes flat it's because I buy the wrong sort of rubber; if a resident or an intern gets a bellyache it's because Walter Carew is too stingy to buy decent food . . . But the point is: Do you think that I can beg or borrow or steal you from Gillespie for this one evening? I mean to say: Will you ask him for the time off?'

Kildare hesitated.

'You have it coming to you,' insisted Carew. 'By a freak of circumstance it becomes highly probable that you could be useful to this institution, Doctor Kildare, if I can dispose of you for one evening. And you have time off coming to you. It's the talk of the whole place that Gillespie works you like a dog—like a dog—day and night—he's making an old man of you.'

'I'd hate to ask him for time off,' said Kildare slowly.

'I know,' nodded Carew. 'You're afraid that he'd blow your head off.'

'No, sir. He'd give me as much time as I want—if I ask him seriously.'

'Now you amaze me!'

'But the fact is that when I'm not here he does the work of two men. He doesn't sleep. He burns himself up. And he's not young, you know.'

A smile appeared on the face of Carew like the twisting grain of a knot in hard wood. 'You take care of him, eh? Run his errands, take his beatings, and love him for the trouble he gives you?'

Kildare said nothing.

'If you'll do nothing about it, I'll try to borrow you myself from Gillespie,' said Carew impatiently, and picked his telephone out of its cradle. He was saying presently: 'There's a bit of work called for outside the hospital, a bit of work that may be important for the hospital's whole future, and the absurdity is that your young intern Kildare seems to be the only man for the job. I want to borrow him from you . . .'

Made electrically thin and sharp, like a far-off rooster in a winter dawn, Kildare heard the voice of Gillespie answering: 'The hospital's whole future is not the slightest damned importance to me. Men are what matter, not machines. You can't have Kildare. That's flat.'

His phone crashed up. Carew, after a sour moment of patience, called again. 'A job well done, such as I have in mind, Leonard,' he said, 'might mean the modernization of our whole laboratory facilities.'

'We haven't any laboratory facilities to modernize!' shouted Gillespie. 'We've nothing but one tin sink and two Bunsen burners. Take Kildare and do what you can with him ... But get him back here fast.'

Carew rang off in a sweat of relief. 'I've got you for this evening, Kildare,' he said, 'and now I want you to make every instant count. Down on the street you'll find a limousine waiting; ask for Mr Messenger's car; go where it takes you ... Kildare, you know about Paul Messenger?'

'No, sir. Only that he's a very rich man.'

'Rich man? There are thousands of rich men, Kildare, but there's only one Messenger. Why, he's the fellow who built the whole observatory at San Jacinto in New Mexico. Millions of dollars to observe the stars ... to observe the infernal stars, mind you, when we're still fighting hand to hand with disease! And now Paul Messenger needs help. I'm not permitted to say one word to you about the case; I can only say that at the present moment Messenger thinks you may be the only man in the world capable of helping him. I say that I can't talk about the case, but I can talk about your manner of approach to it. Doctor Kildare, you are a fellow with an admirable character for honesty and patience and medical insight; but I beg you to remember that there are also qualities such as tact and gentleness of approach and a willingness to favor the other fellow's point of view . . . Hurry along now . . . Every minute may be important . . . But try to remember that out of this case the hospital might receive benefactions so important that its ability to serve the world may be doubled. And you yourself may be founding a rich practice for the future.'

He took Kildare as far as the door of his office, holding his arm in a nervous grip. But even when the door was open, he could not let him go for an instant, repeating: 'Straightforward honesty is an admirable quality—but when in Rome, remember to do as the Romans—and diplomacy has moved mountains in the past, young man—a light touch may do more than a sledge-hammer stroke . . .'

CHAPTER FIVE

Kildare got away at last. He found the Messenger car, driven by a chauffeur with a disdainful manner and a sooty streak of mustache across the upper lip. He took the big automobile swiftly and smoothly through the cross-town traffic and turned up to a Fifth Avenue house. As Kildare got to the pavement, he saw Central Park South rising by lighted stages and towers into the smoke of the autumn evening; the Park itself was lost in a blue fume of twilight as the chauffeur took him to the front door and rang the bell. It was a great door of wrought iron and glass, draped with vaguely translucent curtains inside. A tall old servant opened to Kildare.

'All right, Markham,' said the chauffeur, and this watchword let Kildare enter a hall paved in large black and white marble squares.

'Mr Messenger expects you in the library, sir,' said the butler, and led the way up a stairway flanked by potted, huge azaleas. The red carpet sponged up all the noise of footfalls except a whispering; a hushed expectancy began to grow in Kildare. Through the upper hall the butler brought him into the library, saying: 'Mr Messenger, your guest, sir,' and then closed the door behind him.

Messenger rose from beside the fire. The

glow of it extended over the panels of yellow pine but left under shadow the reds and blues of levant morocco bindings, the ivory of vellum, and the darkening golden brown of pigskin. Two floor lamps clipped out rounds of blue from the rug, yet the room on the whole was left to a restful dusk; and the white hair of Messenger, as he came toward Kildare, seemed to endow him with his own light. He had both a mustache and beard, but clipped as short as though they had to be worn inside a helmet. He was still a huge frame of a man and must have been at one time of tremendous vigor; the last flush of it was in his face, in the bigness of a vein upon his forehead, and the overwhelming boldness of his eye. He continued to stare into Kildare as he took his hand.

His first words were: 'I want you to make a diagnosis without seeing the patient. Can you try that?'

'I can try it,' said Kildare.

'Sit down over here then. Turn your chair a little so that the light gets at your face. When human beings talk they use more than words, and we mustn't be in the dark to one another ... Will you drink?'

'Not now,' said Kildare.

'Are you comfortable and at ease? Is there anything about me or this room that embarrasses you? If so, we'll talk about other things until you're at home.'

'There is no reason why we should waste

time,' replied Kildare.

Messenger, watching his guest, nodded slowly.

'I've heard that you're calm, alert, tenacious in your purposes, and absolutely independent. I begin to feel that all these things are true of you,' he remarked. 'But I also wish that you were ten years older. I've heard a good deal about your discretion, but I know that young tongues are hinged in the middle and wag very easily. I am going to ask for your promise to repeat nothing that you hear from me.'

'Very well,' said Kildare.

Messenger considered this answer for a moment and seemed to find it too casual; but presently he went on: 'I'm going to describe two young women for you. They are my reason for calling you in.'

Kildare took out a small notebook and a pen.

'No,' said Messenger. 'I want to watch your face. The details will remain in your mind. They are not obscure. The first girl I offer for your consideration is twenty years old. She is a type of modern young outdoor America. She can take her horse over the jumps like a professional. If you're no better than the average, she'll outwalk you, outswim you, and give you fifteen and a beating at tennis. Most of the time she wishes for bigger shoulders and narrower hips; as a matter of fact, she almost would prefer to be a man. But she gets on with the lads very well in every way. At a dance she's as popular as the next one. She knows how to take her liquor and how to leave it. She has a talent for friendship. The boys and the girls are constantly around her night and day. At the same time she manages a close and affectionate life with her family. As the poet says, she likes whatever she sees, and her looks go everywhere. Probably she would be called a typical extrovert. Is the picture clear in your mind? I ought to add that she's engaged to as fine a fellow as you could find.'

'Yes,' said Kildare. 'The picture is clear.'

'Now I offer you a picture of the second girl. Outdoor sports are nothing to her. She wouldn't cross the street to see an international polo match. She doesn't like to be alone, and yet out of people she gets only a very vague and dreamy pleasure. She goes to all the night clubs; dancing seems to be the one absorbing passion in her life; neither friends nor family are of the slightest interest to her. A good many young girls grow too fond of night life, but this one uses the night places, not as though she were fond of the nonsense that goes on in them, but as though she needed them to kill time, as a person in pain needs a narcotic ... Is that enough of a picture?'

'No,' said Kildare, 'there are a great many things I'd like to know about the second girl.'

'Ask questions then,' said the big man tersely.

'Do you know about the early life of the second girl? Was it pleasant?'

'Quite. Yes. Quite. But here I've thrown out a quantity of information, and what does the diagnostician's brain say to you about these two girls? Does anything come?'

'It's very serious,' said Kildare, frowning at his host. 'That is to say, it seems serious at the first glance. You yourself have no idea of what may have caused the change?'

'Change? I've said nothing about a change,' said Messenger.

'The change of the first girl into the second,' said Kildare, making a small, impatient gesture.

'Ah,' said Messenger.

He exhaled a long breath and settled back into his chair. 'If you guessed that at the very start,' he declared, 'I think before the end that you may go as far as my friends promise. It's true that I'm talking about only one person—who changed.'

'A daughter?' asked Kildare.

'You might have learned this through other people. What *do* you know about me, Doctor Kildare?'

'I know that you're rich, and that you built an observatory at San Jacinto.'

'Nothing else?'

'Half an hour ago, Doctor Carew was telling me these things. I've never spoken of you before.'

Messenger stood up and made through the room some long and slow measured strides. When he turned in the more distant shadow he looked younger, more formidable, and the swollen vein in his forehead was like a sign of wrath. He was very excited as he said: 'So far you've seen through everything. Don't stop your guesswork now. Go on and tell me more about Nancy.'

'I'll have to see her,' said Kildare, 'and then I'll do what I can, but what you need is not I, but a sound psychiatrist twice my age.'

'I don't think so,' answered Messenger. 'The Chanlers told me what you did for their daughter when older men in the medical profession would have written her off as a mental case. Kildare, I don't want Nancy written off in that way.'

He waited for a comment. Kildare said nothing, but looked down at a bright circle of blue which a floor lamp cut out of the rug. Then the voice of Messenger sounded just above him. He had come swiftly and soundlessly across the room.

'Barbara Chanler disappeared from her home. At that moment she was rich; she had every prospect before her of a happy and well-filled life; her family was devoted to her and she to them; she was about to be married to a man she loved. Then she was picked up as a nameless waif who had tried to commit suicide in a cheap rooming house. A young intern from the hospital answered the emergency call and refused to give her up for dead even when the sheet was pulled over her face. He brought her back to life. In the hospital she tried to take her life a second time. The young intern refused to believe that her mind was gone in spite of these two attempts, and he held on like a bulldog until he'd proven to her that she was wrong about herself and so was the rest of the world.'

Messenger ended his pacing and sat down abruptly in the chair opposite Kildare. His lowered voice said: 'Older minds perhaps would be better for my daughter's case. On the other hand, young people ought to understand other youth by instinct. And above all, I feel that there is a close relationship between the case of Barbara Chanler and that of Nancy.'

'You mean that there was a sudden change in each instance?' asked Kildare. 'Or do you mean that you're afraid your daughter may take her own life?'

The blunt question was by no means an instance of that smooth diplomacy for which Carew had begged when he sent the intern out on this case. Messenger absorbed the shock for a moment before he said: 'This change in my daughter is more than normal. How far beyond normal must I consider it? Is she a mental case requiring isolation? Those are some of the questions I want you to answer.'

'That's impossible until I've had a chance to

see her and study her reactions in detail,' answered Kildare.

'We can't manage that,' said Messenger. 'She's been afraid of doctors for years; it's a real phobia in her. If she's in a critical mental state and finds out that I'm using a doctor to spy on her, she may be driven frantic and then—I keep Barbara Chanler in mind.'

A murmur of voices from the lower part of the house got Messenger hastily out of his chair again. 'That's Nancy now,' he said.

'Why not introduce me as a friend, not as a doctor?' asked Kildare.

'And then have the truth come out to bite us?'

'No one in New York knows me except the Chanlers, and they're not in town now. Give me another name. I'm John Stevens—from the West somewhere. You knew my father in the old days.'

'It's melodrama. It's absurd,' murmured Messenger. He pulled open the door a trifle so that the voices entered, small but clear. The girl was saying: 'But I don't want you to, Charles. I don't want to drag you around. You go home and get your sleep.'

Messenger, listening, turned his head sharply, and Kildare saw the vein in his forehead again, like a sign of wrath which did not go with the glistening fear in the eyes. He came back toward the fire again.

'Are you busy, father? May we come in?'

asked Nancy at the door.

Messenger looked fixedly at Kildare.

'Come in, come in!' he called, and as Kildare stood up, Nancy Messenger entered, throwing open her coat and smiling back over her shoulder at her companion. Every feature of her appearance had to have meaning to Kildare, as though he were a portrait painter. He remembered a picture of that great lover and termagant, Sarah, the first Duchess of Marlborough, for the girl had somewhat the same look of resolute and forward pride and the same soft fullness of lips which somehow suggested willful determination rather than feminine gentleness. She had something of her father, in miniature, and as she grew older the resemblance would be greater; she even had the vein in the forehead, though in her it was merely a pale stroke of blue.

Messenger was saying: 'Nancy, this is John Stevens, a son of an old friend of mine . . . and this is Charles Herron.'

Herron was one of those broad-beamed man-mountains who are useful at tackle in the football line to spill the whole charge of a backfield. He was a bit past thirty, and he was somewhat overweighted by the inevitable extra poundings that is bound to accumulate on a very strong man. His width made his height unapparent until he came up close to shake hands.

Nancy, after a brief smile of greeting, had

found nothing in Kildare and obviously dismissed him from her thoughts.

'Now I'm safely home, Charles, and you can go get your sleep,' she said. She added to her father: 'There's so much of him that when he's tired it's a tremendous ache.'

'I'm too heavy for this long-distance running,' remarked Herron. 'Three nights and three afternoons and she's still full of go. I suppose you'll be out again tonight, Nancy?'

'Oh, no. I don't think so.'

'You will, though ... She thinks that if she keeps going where the lights are the brightest she'll see something worth while.'

He tried to maintain a certain lightness of touch, but it was plain that he was deeply troubled. He kept looking from the girl to her father as though he might find an explanation by making a detailed comparison.

'Blame her for being young. That includes being silly,' suggested Messenger.

'I want you to promise me something, Nancy. Will you?' asked Herron.

'He's a lawyer, and he makes a living out of broken promises,' said the girl, laughing. 'Don't be that way, Charles, please!'

'It's not a great thing, but I'm curious. Can you stay home for a single evening, Nancy?'

He was bearing down on his point much too heavily, particularly with a stranger in the room, but he was too disturbed to be diplomatic. Messenger could not hide the concern with which he watched the two of them. Nancy went up to Herron and shone her eyes at him exactly as though they had been a thousand miles from observation. It was clear that she wanted this man and did not care if the whole world knew about her choice.

'Of *course* I can stay home if you want me to,' she said. 'But don't be such an old, *old* man, Charles. There's a lot of living to do.'

'Not in these night spots,' said Herron, 'getting sticky with cocktails and dizzy with champagne and listening to the crooners wail. Why don't you quit it, Nancy?'

'I'm going to pretty soon,' she said. 'You run along home while you're still nice and sour, and I'll telephone to you in half an hour when you're in bed. I'll talk you to sleep, Charles.'

She led him across the room.

'It's a go then,' he said. 'I'm going to be able to think of you spending one quiet evening at home?'

'Of course you can think of me that way.'

'You won't let something steal you?'

'I won't be kidnapped.'

He made an odd gesture that Kildare never forgot, extending his hand a little past her, as though he were trying to keep some danger away. When he spoke, it was only for her, but the natural bigness of his voice carried the words in a murmur across the room. 'I don't know,' he said. 'Every time I'm with you lately I feel that I'll never see you again.'

'Charles! Don't say such a thing!' whispered the girl.

'I shouldn't say it. Forgive me, Nancy,' said the murmuring, deep voice.

Kildare turned his head sharply and looked out of the window. It was true that he was in the house as a physician to make inquiry into the state of a patient, but now he felt like an eavesdropper. It was as though he had peeped through a keyhole and seen big Charles Herron weeping, unmanned.

Herron went out hastily. The girl, starting to go down with him, changed her mind. She stood for a moment at the open door hesitant, fighting out a quick, earnest battle in her mind. It was as though she were tempted to hurry after Herron and say something more. Kildare felt the eyes of big Messenger fixed upon him, urging him, in the silence, to consider this moment as a piece of important psychological evidence. As a matter of fact he could add up a number of interesting items, but the chief of all was that Nancy Messenger loved Herron no matter how she allowed her way of living to displease him.

'I'm going up to change for dinner,' said Nancy, and went out with her head still thoughtfully bent. The door closed behind her soundlessly, as though she were in fear of making a noise.

CHAPTER SIX

To Kildare, lost in thought, the voice of Messenger came eagerly, saying: 'How does it seem to you, Kildare?'

'It doesn't make sense,' answered Kildare, frowning at the fire.

'It's a puzzle, of course,' said Messenger, 'but I hoped that you might arrive at something about Nancy. You've seen the two largest factors in her life—her past in me, her present and future in Herron. Doesn't some light fall on the problem?'

'Light? There's too much light,' said Kildare. 'There's enough of it to blind me. The sort of light that shows one the solution in a psychological case like this is usually a single ray, not a whole flood.'

'For a man in doubt, you're saying a great deal. You're calling it a psychological case at once. You're dismissing the possibility that her sudden change in the way of living is simply a natural desire to see a great deal of the world before she settles down in marriage.'

'Yes, I'm dismissing that possibility,' said Kildare gloomily.

'Will you give me some of the reasons?'

'You know most of them. Herron is one.'

'Charles Herron?'

'A man in love doesn't see things with

ordinary eyes, and what he sees in her frightens him badly. He can't live without her; but he's afraid that he'll have to try before long.'

'You've only had a glimpse of them,' said Messenger curiously, 'but you think it's a grand passion?'

'I think it is,' said Kildare.

'At least,' said Messenger, 'you have the advantage of a quiet evening's talk with her, because she'll be staying home tonight.'

'I don't think so,' said Kildare, shaking his head.

'My dear fellow,' said Messenger, 'you heard Herron directly ask her to stay in, didn't you? You've already told me how much they mean to one another. No matter how headstrong she may be, she couldn't disregard as direct and strong a request as this.'

'Nevertheless, I think she will.'

'That's impossible—if she loves Herron.'

'I think she'll do anything rather than spend a single evening in this house.'

'You can't be sure of that!' declared Messenger.

'I wish I were never less sure of anything,' answered the intern.

'Do you think there's some profound reaction against her home? Might it be a revulsion against me?'

'I hope not. I don't know.'

Messenger put up his hand and dragged it slowly down over his face.

'Let's get it down to words of one syllable: You think that Nancy will leave the house this evening?'

'She will,' said Kildare. 'And when she goes, you must try to hitch me to her.'

'She can't leave. She has Herron's very strong injunct against it. She's promised. She knows that Herron is not a fellow whose wish can be bandied about lightly.'

'No. She doesn't take him lightly,' agreed Kildare. 'But she has to go.'

'But where? Into the nonsense of the night clubs again? What do they mean to her?'

'Nothing, probably.'

'Then why in God's name should she go to them? Doctor Kildare, I'm trying to understand you.'

'I'm trying to understand myself,' said Kildare. 'But there's only a vague light to see by. In a case like this, there's no use straining the eyes. A glimpse will probably tell more than a microscope. We have to wait for some accidental clue—perhaps something she says; perhaps not the words, but the way she speaks them. It may be something as small as a color she likes or shrinks from. Detectives and their crimes—they have an easy time of it—they have a blood stain—or a body—or a weapon; they have motives printed large enough to serve as headlines. But a case like this—why, she probably doesn't know what drives her to act as she's acting now. If I dared to ask her direct questions, I doubt that she'd be able to give me the answers even if she wanted to.'

The door was pulled open and Nancy stood on the threshold in a white jacket over a black dress with a flaring, pleated skirt. A double round of big pearls shimmered at her throat.

'Hello and good-by! I've had a call!' she cried, waving to them.

'Wait a minute! Nancy!' exclaimed the father as the door began to close again.

'Yes?' she called, looking back for an instant.

'Take John Stevens along with you.'

'Oh, I'd be glad to. But it's not my party. It's Harry Wendell...'

'Wendell? You can't go out with people like the Wendells, my dear!'

'Oh, yes. In *this* country I can,' she answered, laughing a little.

'Very well. But add John Stevens to the Wendell party ... Sorry to let you mix with such a crowd of bounders, but go along, John. It will be better than glooming through an evening alone with me. Be nice to him, Nancy. He's worth an effort—if you're really going out. You haven't forgotten what Herron said, have you?'

'Charles?' she winced. It was almost a shudder, and her eyes closed. Then she said briskly: 'Shall we be starting on? We're late, Mr Stevens.'

Messenger, following on to the door, stuffed

into the coat pocket of Kildare a stiff sheaf of money; then the two of them were hurrying down the hall, Nancy saying with an unhappy attempt at lightness: 'I don't need to worry about Charles Herron, do I? When a lawyer expects to be taken seriously, he sends a court order or a summons, doesn't he?'

She was stating a theory, not asking a question, so Kildare did not have to answer.

However, he said: 'Lawyers are always dealing with facts; overt acts mean a lot to them, don't they?'

She stopped short. She had been hard-hit by his remark, but after an instant she shrugged it off and went on.

The limousine picked them up and slid them away through the traffic.

'How far away in the West do you live?' asked Nancy, leaning back into her corner and yawning a little.

'Not as far as California,' answered Kildare.

'Some place where there are trails to ride, or canoes and white water and log-jams and things worth while?'

'No. Just another big town.'

She nodded as if to say that she had expected as much. When her eyes glanced away from him again, he knew that he was forgotten.

'Shall I be spoiling a party? Shall I be breaking in on a lot of old friends?' he asked.

'It's up to you,' she said indifferently. 'If you can put up with the party, the party can put up with you. Isn't that usually the way of it?'

It was worse than insolence, this insouciance. It stifled him above all with its unexpectedness, and he knew at once that she was not fully aware of what she had said. Sick people think chiefly of their own concerns.

She hardly spoke another word to him, and Kildare at every traffic stop found himself automatically searching the sidewalk crowd for the great shoulders and the strong, handsome face of Charles Herron; he was sure to find out about this broken promise. Then they were shooting up in a soundless, luxurious private elevator and walking into an apartment that made a point of spreading its elbows.

Harry Wendell came from a distance, calling out, making a gesture of triumph over Nancy.

'Everything is going to be beautiful now,' he said, 'except that Liz Baker is here and already as tight as an owl.'

'That's all right. Mr Stevens is from the Far West where they know how to take care of the wild things. Show Liz to him, and he'll control her.'

'I thank God for you, Nancy,' said Wendell. 'I thank God for you and all your works. Come on and get a load of Liz, Stevens.'

The ballroom was as vaulted and almost as big as Grand Central Station. At one end of it a large orchestra was playing industriously. Quantities of young America slithered here and there in couples, but Liz Baker, young and dark and beautiful, was draped over one end of a blue couch studying her blurred image in the polished floor.

'If that's water,' said Liz, 'I'm going to drown myself.'

'Here's an old pal of yours from the Great West,' said Mr Wendell. 'He'll help you make yourself at home. Give her a hand, John.'

'What Johnny are you?' asked Liz. 'And how far west are you, and what are you west of? I'm so full of great open spaces that my head is spinning and I can't find those mint juleps. Come on and help me find them, Johnny.'

She got up and shook herself. Her tousled hair sprang back into shape like untangling springs.

'I can't walk, but I can dance,' said Liz.

They danced across shining acres until Liz heard the rattle of ice in cocktail shakers and the chime of glasses jingling on a tray.

'You can't dance, but maybe you can walk,' said Liz. 'Try to find that sound and bring me some of it. I don't mean the music, sweet.'

He helped her toward the bartenders. He did not trouble about her because he knew that young Liz Baker already was beyond doctor's care.

'Is this a silver dress I'm wearing, or am I frosted?' she asked.

'That's a silver dress you're wearing,' said Kildare.

'If I had something green in my hair, I'd look like a mint julep, but that's not the way I feel. There's more mint than there is julep about me, honey, if that means anything. Bartender, does that mean anything?'

'That means a whole heap,' said the bartender. 'If you were to take and lay down with a lump of ice on the back of your neck, you'd feel a lot more like a mint julep than you do now. Here's some mint for her,' said the bartender, offering a green bit of it to Kildare.

'That's right, give him that sprig of mint,' said Liz. 'That's what he needs when he dances. There's no sprig in him. Does that hurt your feelings, darling? Does it hurt him, bartender?'

'You can't tell about a thinking man,' suggested the bartender.

'Why should he think? Why should he be as mean as all that?' asked Liz Baker. 'Listen, Johnny, why do you want to go around thinking all over the place? Honey, I don't need you any more. I don't need anyone when I'm this close to the cracked ice. Hey—somebody come and take Johnny. You don't have to pay. I'll give him away.'

Kildare drifted off. The rooms were filling. An endless chain of servants began to serve dinner from a great buffet. Alternate trays of drinks and food journeyed through the apartment. He found Wendell and said: 'I'm sorry that I couldn't handle Liz Baker.'

'What do you mean you couldn't handle

her? You're wonderful,' declared the host. 'Liz has to drop some place, and it's best to have her over there near the service entrance . . . Where's your drink?'

He dodged a drink. As a matter of fact it was easy for him to do as he pleased in such a crowd, so he kept drifting, passing into little pools and shallows of conversation now and then, and then moving on again so that he could keep Nancy Messenger in sight. She obviously was different from these people, and as she wandered about with an air of abstraction and a vague smile that kept them at arm's length, they seemed glad to have her, but hardly to know what to do about her. It was equally obvious that for mysterious reasons she was glad to be in the place. Then, just after eleven, she almost disappeared from him in the midst of a group who were leaving. He managed to get into the elevator with them.

'I didn't know it was time to go,' he said to Nancy.

'It isn't,' answered Nancy. 'It's never time to go, unless you want to. You're not going to have me on your conscience, are you?'

Then she forgot him again. They went to a night club, and on the way Nancy, with her usual indifference, introduced him only to one member of the group, a Charlotte Fothergill who was plump and pretty and equipped with an inextinguishable smile.

'Charlotte, this is a son of a friend of my

father's. He comes from out West,' said Nancy. 'She's a great horsewoman, John.'

'Those great big ranches out West are wonderful,' said Charlotte. 'How many hundred square miles are there in your ranch, Mr Stevens?'

'I haven't a ranch,' said Kildare.

'I mean, the kind they have down in Texas,' said Charlotte Fothergill. 'You ride for days and days and get lost. How many times have you been lost on your ranch, Johnny?'

'I haven't a ranch,' said Kildare.

'I mean, not really lost, but not knowing where you are,' said Charlotte. 'I was lost in a department store once. I had to buy my way out of the lingerie department, and before I got clear I had enough to last me the rest of my life. And then the styles all changed and there I was. It was frightful ... Dingie, here's a man after your own heart, with a thousand square miles of ranch down in Texas. Johnny, this is Hugh Dingwell. Dingie has a place down in the Tennessee Valley Authority, but he goes in for Grand Rapids furniture and that's a pity, don't you think?'

'Charlotte is just a little twisted,' said Dingwell, who was a tall young man with a pinched face and nervous lips. 'I have a place down in Tennessee and most of my horses are out of the Rapidan line. You know—Rapidan, who got Rapid Waters, who got Rap Me—but what are you breeding in the way of horseflesh on your ranch?'

'I haven't a ranch,' said Kildare.

'I know you fellows,' said Dingwell. 'Anything less than a hundred thousand acres doesn't count. I know a lot of fellows out Texas way that use the Irish Boy strain. If they're not big enough to race, they're big enough for polo, so there you are, and you can't lose. Missionary came from out there. You know Missionary, don't you?'

'I never heard of him,' said Kildare.

Dingwell laughed, but it was easy to see that he was hurt.

'Light in the forehand, I grant you that, and some of his get let you down beyond a mile. But I wouldn't say that I'd never *heard* of Missionary. They broke his back with weight in the Belmont or you know what would have happened. And then he got Salvation out of Jingle Bells, and you can't laugh off Salvation, can you? Jacqueline, here's a fellow who owns half of Texas, and he wouldn't have Missionary blood on his place. Not for a gift, he wouldn't.'

Jacqueline turned her head slowly and looked Kildare up and down. 'How naive!' she said. 'What *would* you use? Domingo, perhaps?'

'Why not Domingo?' asked Dingwell. 'Look at Dominic and Do-Re-Mi, both chuck a block with Domingo blood.'

'Domingo horses are front runners and

nothing else,' said Jacqueline with decision. 'The dirty dogs drop dead in the stretch if anything comes up and looks them in the eye. Uncle Tom, I want you to talk to John Stevens here; he has a million acres of Texas all full of that lousy Domingo strain...'

This chatter continued from the automobile into the night club, until the Fothergill girl said: 'Nancy, whatever made you sell that mare of yours? "Distinction," wasn't that her name? What did you go and sell that mare for last month? I thought you were sure crazy about that little old chestnut jumper.'

The whole group of these horsy people turned on Nancy with voluble questions, and Kildare saw that she was badly hurt. A signal from her brought them out dancing together, and as they danced she said: 'I've got to get away. This talk about horses, horses, is driving me crazy. Get me away from them, John?'

They slipped away during an act of the floor show that came on.

'Are we stopping or going on?' she asked.

'I wish we were never stopping,' said Kildare. 'I mean, I hate to see things stop.'

She looked with a sudden flash of interest at him—and they went on. Wherever they went somebody knew her, a party seemed ready to engulf her, yet she never seemed fully aware of what was going on around her. She drank little, danced a great deal, and in her face there appeared, it seemed to Kildare, greater and greater apprehension, as though she were approaching some invisible danger. At four o'clock, when the wheels that make New York travel by night all stop, Nancy Messenger bought the whole orchestra for triple pay and took it with a dozen of the last guests at the night club to a little apartment belonging to one of these new friends. There the party started all over again with a whoop, but the enthusiasm could not last. Dancing weariness and alcoholic fatigue began to reduce them to sleep by five-thirty. At six the party crumbled away to nothing and left Kildare with Nancy in the limousine which the chauffeur with the black streak of mustache was driving. She had been working hard up to the very moment when the party fell to pieces, like a driver whipping on tired horses, but she could not keep that group awake. Now she sat back with her eyes closed, apparently exhausted, but still he noted a certain tremulous tension about her lips.

'Tell me where to take you,' said the girl, without opening her eyes. 'Where are you staying?'

'I suppose I have to be dropped somewhere,' agreed Kildare. 'I don't suppose we just could drive on for a while.'

He had his elbows on his knees and stared straight ahead, but he could feel the girl wake up beside him.

'We can have a spin through the Park, if you

want,' she said.

'That's better than nothing,' nodded Kildare. 'Let's do that.'

So the car was turned up Fifth Avenue and then in at the Sixtieth Street entrance.

CHAPTER SEVEN

He knew that before the single round of the Park had been completed he must do his work with the girl. If he failed to hold her now, she was gone through his fingers. Still he could not find a good approach. In the hospital things were not like this. Patients had to answer questions there, but even a single interrogation probably would close the lips of Nancy for the rest of the night. When he tried to think his way forward, he found his train of thought dissipating among the clouds of frosty trees that swept away behind them, left and right; when he searched for words, the hollow of his brain was filled by the rushing noise of the tires over the wet pavement, like a high wind. They continually were slowing for a red light, gathering soft way again when the green appeared. They were up by the reservoir and still the silence held Kildare. Ahead of them he saw a big yellow street lamp like a rising moon or a sun through heavy mist.

'The long nights,' said Kildare. 'Now—if

that were the sun coming up—you know?'

He glanced nervously toward her and found that she was appraising him with a coldly curious eye. She was interested, but from a great distance. However, he had struck out a line and for lack of a better he stuck to it. 'I thought it would be worse than this, though,' said Kildare. 'I mean, about two o'clock it looked to me as though the party was going smash.'

'Well, would that have been such a great disaster?' she asked.

'No, not to you, of course,' said Kildare. He reached into his memory of certain cases and found phrases ready-made at his hand. 'You don't know anything about the emptiness that spins like a wheel, do you?'

'Emptiness—spins?' she repeated. She sat up and looked at him.

'I don't want to talk about it. It's horrible,' said Kildare. 'But I mean—the darkness whistling—I'm not making any sense, am I?'

'I don't mind listening,' she told him.

'You'd mind if I told you more about it, though,' went on Kildare. 'The room you've been living in all day, happily enough—you've never had that room turn into a coffin when the night comes, have you?' A sudden movement of her head told him that he had caught her full attention at last, but she was silent. He leaned back and put a hand over his face. In this way he covered his smile of triumph, but also he felt like a sneak-thief. He said: 'The right sort of people go to bed at a decent time, and they never stir until the daylight comes. But there are other people who'd rather have a hangman fit a noose around their neck than be alone at night.—Do you mind me talking?'

When she spoke to him now, there was a softening of her voice that gave a new quality to the whole night. 'Does it help you to talk about it?' she asked. 'I'm glad to listen.'

'May I?' asked Kildare with a pretended eagerness. 'Sometimes talking about it—if only one can find the right person—makes the whole business seem as childish as Mother Goose. It *is* childish, isn't it?'

'Fear of the dark?' she asked.

'*You* don't know anything about it,' declared Kildare, rousing himself to a greater fervor. 'I can tell the people who never have any trouble about the night. They have clean, clear eyes like yours. They've never gone to sleep and dreamed that they were buried alive. They've never had a dream like that. Shall I tell you what it's like?'

'Yes—tell me,' she said. He could feel her tension. It was like having a fish on a line.

'There are twenty different kinds,' said Kildare. 'One of them is like this: You're lying down on a smooth green lawn stretched out under a tree that makes a sort of a green heaven over you. The blue of the sky filters down through the branches till you know that you're asleep. It's the sort of a sleep that children have, perfect unconsciousness and a sense of being carried along toward happiness. There's a bit of a wind blowing, and after a while it drifts over the grass a ripple of sand, a harmless little ripple of sand. It rolls up; it breaks and barely tickles your skin. Another ripple comes with the wind. The sand fits cool and snug under your cheek. More ripples build the sand higher and higher around your face … You can't move, you know. The sleep has bound you down like cold irons. You can't stir, and the sand is up to your lips now. If you dare to open your mouth, it will pour down your throat. It reaches your nostrils. All at once—my God, you're breathing the sand into your lungs! All the clean air with life in it is gone from the world!'

'Don't go on! Stop!' whispered Nancy.

He pretended not to hear, continuing as though horribly entranced. 'Then you wake up. The darkness is like the sand. It stifles your lungs. A scream builds up high in your throat. You snap on the light and you see your own room there about you—your clothes on a chair perhaps, and your book on the table and everything as familiar as a painting. That's it. It's only a painting. It's all dead, and you're dead with it and in it. You'll never get outside that frame into the living world where the air can be breathed. If you're lucky, maybe you don't scream, but you jump out of the bed and run to the window. You fall on your knees and lean out in the night. You tell yourself that it's only a dream. But the horror won't leave, and your heart is going crazy. You gasp and bite at the air. There's no taste of life in it. The whole world is darkness or else a few little funeral lights along the street to show you it's a city of the dead with nothing but the black of the night to breathe...'

'I can't stand it,' cried Nancy.

He got out a handkerchief and dragged it across his forehead. He scrubbed the wet from his face, up and down, as one poor devil always had done in the hospital.

'I shouldn't have talked about it,' said Kildare huskily. 'It's like a ghost story, and it'll give you the horrors. Only—I want you to understand what it means—to some of us—to be alone at night and to fall asleep in the dark and wake up throttled by the blackness. Are you going to forgive me for telling you all this?'

'Forgive you?' said the girl. 'Don't you see? That's what sleep means to me!'

He had expected to be triumphant if he caught her in his trap, but all that he felt was a stroke of profound pity.

'D'you mean that *you* have been that way?' he said, as though surprised.

'Why else was I herding around with swine tonight? Johnny, if you look at me I know that you can see the horror in my eyes. I can feel them like shadows of apes here in the corners of my brain.'

He looked straight into the staring of her eyes. She needed comforting, like a child, but that could not be his role. He had to diagnose before he could cure.

'I know,' said Kildare.

'Is there the same feeling in you, Johnny?'

'It's exactly the same,' he said.

'Then I'm not going crazy? It can't be insanity if two of us have the same imaginings?'

'Of course it can't,' said Kildare.

'Sometimes even having people in the room doesn't help, does it?' she went on.

'Not a bit.'

'They're like ghosts, not flesh and blood. There's a dreadful graveyard sense of darkness and decay and horrible death . . .'

Her voice had not grown louder, but her face looked like screaming. Kildare put an arm around her. She pushed at him with her hands.

'You get that jitter out of you,' he said.

'It'll never go; it'll never leave me,' said Nancy Messenger. 'It's going to throttle me some night; it's going to drive me out the window into the street; it's going to kill me, Johnny.'

'It can't do that now,' said Kildare. 'We've found one another. We can put up a fight together because we understand.'

'Could I call you when things get bad?'

'Day or night.'

'And you won't mind?'

'Mind? I'll be going through the same thing probably.'

'If we've got each other, Johnny, we *can* fight off the horrors, can't we?... Poor Johnny, poor boy! What was it that started the dreadfulness in you? But I mustn't ask.'

'Why not?' he demanded, trying to keep the eagerness out of his voice, for he saw that he was on the verge of making the great discovery. 'I'll tell you all about what started it in me.'

She shook her head violently, her eyes closed to keep out the very thought.

'No, we'll never ask questions,' she insisted. 'Then there'll never have to be any horrible answering.'

He saw that it would be foolish to keep on; but there was a silent groan in his throat when he realized how close he had come to the secret.

'Look—over there to the right!'

'I see them—those black clouds, you mean?' she said.

She held close to Kildare as though she hardly dared to face a moment in the world without him.

'Of course they're black because the sun is rising behind them, Nancy. The day's beginning, and we can put this one night behind us.'

Her head dropped back against his shoulder.

'You'll stay with me, Johnny, will you?'

'Yes,' he promised.

'You won't let them take you away from

New York?'

'I'm going to stay here where I can find you when things go black for me.'

'You'll stay with me, Johnny, till the end? Promise me, promise me! It won't be long. I'm going to finish it all; but promise me to stay till the end?'

CHAPTER EIGHT

Kildare wakened from a dream of sinful delay and mountainous defeat. His eyes refused to recognize the big four-poster in which he lay. He felt for an instant as though some reshuffling of time had dealt him into a far-off country. The tall figure in the doorway with the white, close-clipped beard and mustache was a perfect part of the illusion of the past for an instant, then he was sitting up and saying good morning to Paul Messenger.

'Go back to sleep,' said Messenger, smiling. 'Doctor Carew has been on the telephone with me from the hospital to say that a certain Gillespie has been asking for you; and I've told Carew that you're not to be disturbed. I've only looked in on you to tell you that everything is all right. Go back to sleep and get your rest.'

The sleep which was stagnating his brain gradually cleared away. From the speech of

Paul Messenger he retained one singular phrase: 'a certain Gillespie.'

'Have you never heard of Dr Leonard Gillespie?' he asked, bewildered.

'No,' said Messenger, 'but I've seen Nancy, and I've heard enough from her to realize that the Chanlers were right and that you are the man for this work. She speaks of you with real affection, Kildare. She talks almost as though you were a brother.'

He came towards the bed, smiling. 'I began to think that no one in the world ever could win her confidence. Herron failed; I failed; but you have the special talent. You're already inside her mind, and I know that you'll get at the root of everything that's wrong.'

The comprehension of Kildare fumbled at these words and made nothing of them. There was only one prime consideration: Gillespie was calling for him, and he was not at hand.

'Will you tell me the time, please?' he asked.

'It's only ten; you've hardly begun to sleep,' answered Messenger.

Kildare stumbled out of the bed and stood up in blue pajamas much too large for him.

'I should have been there at least an hour ago!' he exclaimed.

'My dear fellow, forget the hospital,' said Messenger. 'I'll make everything perfectly all right for you there.'

'Nobody can make things all right for me there. Gillespie—but you haven't even heard of him?'

'One of Carew's subordinates?' asked Messenger, only mildly interested.

'Subordinate?' echoed Kildare. 'If you piled ten Carews and ten hospitals one on top of the other you wouldn't have what Gillespie means. And he'll raise the devil with me for being off duty.'

He tossed off the pajamas and started reaching for his clothes.

'I don't understand this,' said Messenger. 'No matter what the hospital may be, it performs certain services for certain considerations. I'll give them such considerations in return for your time that everyone will be happy. Let me do the worrying about that, please!'

Kildare was jamming himself into his clothes. He panted out the words: 'Can't you understand? Gillespie—but you've never heard of him?'

Messenger said, a little sternly because he felt that too much time was being given to a mere detail: 'Whatever Doctor Gillespie may be, he is a man who serves society and receives compensation for his services. That is axiomatic in the life of every man except saints, and saints are a little out of date, aren't they?'

As he thought of how completely all axioms were worthless in a definition of Gillespie, Kildare made a gesture of surrender. He said: 'Gillespie never took a penny in his life. He'd rather give the world one specific cure than have a whole mountain of gold.'

Kildare was sitting down now rapidly lacing his shoes. Messenger had lost some of his surety.

'I almost take it that you'd walk out of this case if Gillespie whistled you back,' he suggested.

Kildare, whipping on a necktie and knotting it, answered: 'He's the master, and I'm the apprentice. Of course I come when he whistles.'

'Do I take it that you look forward with pleasant expectation to a penniless life like his?' asked Messenger.

'If I could steal a quarter of what he knows, what would money mean?' demanded Kildare, astonished in his turn.

He brushed his fingers through his hair and brought it into rough order. Without a glance at a mirror to check details he was ready to go. For an instant they stared at one another across a distance immeasurably great. Messenger, stricken by the new idea, said suddenly: 'If I can't buy help from you people, can I beg it? That seems the only thing to do!'

'I'll tell you what I know, what I guess, and what I advise you to do,' said Kildare, pulling a thick wad of money from his pocket. 'By the way, here's what's left of what you gave me last night.'

'Damn the money,' snapped Messenger. 'In *your* world, it seems that damning is all that money's good for. Keep the change, will you? What I gave you was nothing.'

'Interns can't accept pay,' answered Kildare a little impatiently.

The reluctant hand of Messenger accepted the bills.

Kildare went on: 'Nancy is the victim of an acute hysteria that takes its form in fear of the night and of being alone. That's what I know definitely. There is something in her mind so horrible that she can't think or speak about it. That's all I know. My guess is that the source of her fear is not in you or Herron. She leaves the house to avoid loneliness. Her dread, I think, is of something in the future. What I advise is that you get the finest psychiatrist and let him work out the problem. In the meantime, let her have her way in everything and be as patient as you can.'

'Kildare, if you knew Nancy better you would understand that she'll never submit to a doctor's care.'

'It's a difficulty,' agreed Kildare. 'But a fine psychiatrist could be introduced as a friend in the house, as I was.'

'He would be someone of name and established reputation. If Nancy didn't recognize him, one of her friends would be sure to. Great scientists are not great actors. Besides, the touch of a middle-aged practitioner would be too heavy and clumsy, probably. She's built a wall that shuts out the rest of the world. By the grace of God and your own devices you've managed to get inside that wall. I'm afraid that nobody else on earth can do that, and now you tell me that you're leaving us in the lurch!'

Kildare thought back to the staring eyes of Nancy. He had to take a great breath to maintain his resolute purpose.

'I'm sorry about her,' he said, 'but I can't stay.'

The face of Messenger glistened with a fine perspiration. He kept a hard hold on himself.

'Let me ask another question,' he said. 'Kildare, don't you feel that with a bit of time you might be able to get at the root of her trouble?'

'I feel that I might, with luck.'

'And don't you feel that there's need for haste?'

Kildare was silent.

'I mean,' went on Messenger, 'won't you agree that in her present state of mind she easily might become desperate?'

'Yes,' said Kildare reluctantly.

'And if she becomes desperate, she would be capable of almost any action?'

'Yes,' said Kildare.

A silence grew up in the room like a field of high electric tension.

At last Kildare said: 'Doctor Gillespie is working now at an experiment that may save thousands of lives. He needs me. I can't imagine anything in the world that would induce him to let me go.'

'Nevertheless,' said Messenger, 'I'll see what can be done to provide the inducement.'

He went out of the room with Kildare and down the stairs beside him. When they came to the front door, they shook hands.

'I know part of the hard thoughts you're thinking,' said Kildare. 'And if it weren't that I'm bound to Gillespie, I'd give anything I know to help Nancy. She means a lot to me.'

'I believe you,' said Messenger solemnly. 'I have no hard thoughts. Every man has his own conception of his duty to others and to himself, but I feel that I shall have you back here on her case before another day has come round.'

Out on the street Kildare found a gusty wind and rain that iced the pavement, but it seemed pleasant weather compared with the unhappiness which he had left behind him. From the corner he looked back at the succession of dignified façades standing shoulder to shoulder with insuperable dignity, each as like the other as so many tall brothers. He turned from them hastily, for the thought of Nancy Messenger came suddenly like a sweet ghost and let the cold of the morning breathe into him.

CHAPTER NINE

When he got to the hospital, he raced to his room and hurried into whites. The brazen voice of the loudspeaker was roaring before he had laced his shoes: 'Calling Doctor Kildare; report at Doctor Carew's office. Calling Doctor Kildare; report at Doctor Carew's office. Calling Doctor Kildare...'

He was out in the corridor with the third repetition still resounding in the room behind him and went at once to the head of the hospital. Carew, biting off the end of a cigar, recognized him with a grunt and a nod as though he were a very distasteful sight. The superintendent, instead of addressing Kildare, preferred to give his attention to the gray mist beyond the windows through which the towers of Manhattan were lifting to an unhappy height.

'I've just had two or three million dollars on the telephone,' he said, letting the smoke issue with his speaking breath and so curl up into his grim face. 'Two or three million hospital dollars; enough to bring this old institution to life; enough to put hundreds of new beds into the service of the poor... I suppose you know what I'm talking about?'

'Mr Messenger?' suggested Kildare.

'Well,' said Carew, 'I don't expect the future

of the hospital to mean much to you, but I wonder if you've thought clearly of all this from your own personal angle? You know that a doctor with clients like the Messengers is bound to get all that money can buy?'

'I'm not thinking of that,' said Kildare, 'but if Doctor Gillespie could be persuaded to let me go for a short time, I think I could help Nancy Messenger.'

'Bah!' said Carew. 'He can't be persuaded. I wouldn't be fool enough to try persuasion. But you could make yourself a free agent, young Doctor Kildare.'

'And give up the work with Doctor Gillespie?'

'And what does that mean? He says you have talent. Very well. And he's willing to teach you. Very well. But the finest memory in the world and the best teaching may not make you another Gillespie . . .'

'I'm not fool enough to hope to be another Gillespie,' said Kildare.

'You hope to be at least half of him. Is that enough for you? Well, it's your own business,' snapped Carew. 'Glory is more than gold, eh? Mind you, I wouldn't usually tempt you away from the strait and narrow . . . But I've already wasted too much time on a hopeless case. Good day, my very young friend.'

So, with a great door closed upon opportunity, Kildare hurried down to the familiar offices of Gillespie. He found Nurse

Cavendish putting things in order while the sea-lion roar of Gillespie resounded vaguely from the adjoining room.

'Are things bad, Molly?' he asked.

'How can they ever be good with him when you stay away and let him work all night?' demanded the Cavendish savagely. 'How can they ever be good when there's only a small bit of life left to him and he pours it out like water on you?'

'On me?' echoed Kildare.

'What else is he doing but giving half of his time and strength to the teaching of you?' exclaimed Molly Cavendish.

'It's true,' agreed Kildare. The nature of that truth took the breath suddenly and cruelly out of him. 'He's wasting himself on me—and on the experiment.'

'Damn the experiment,' said Molly. 'He'd never have grown curious about the meningitis in the first place except you began asking questions that excited him. What would a young man do but make an old man ambitious, anyway?' She concluded in a growl: 'It was a sad day . . . It was a sad day for him when he met . . .'

She did not need to complete the gloomy sentence; Kildare understood the implication perfectly. For that matter, it was not the first time that Molly had showed her ugly temper to him and he had forgiven her because of that deathless devotion which she had offered, for so many years, to the great Gillespie. The rest of the world praised him, but only the Cavendish served him night or day.

'Didn't he sleep last night?' asked Kildare.

'How would he sleep,' cried Molly, 'when things began to go wrong with the damned white mice, and you weren't here to help with them? There's no one else whose hands he trusts, and you know it. How would he have a chance when you go off gadding and leave the poor man alone?'

Kildare slowly turned the knob of the inner door and pushed it open in time to hear Gillespie shout: 'Not file 117D; file 117T is what I want, if you'll open your ears and try to hear what I say to you!'

Mary Lamont, on her knees beside a great drawer jammed full of cards five by eight which contained the complicated records of the experiment, flashed up at Kildare a wild look from a haggard face. If there had been no sleep for Gillespie, it was plain that there had been none for her.

Gillespie was roaring: 'Hurry, hurry! It's passing the time now for the new injection and how in God's name can we vary the compound if the record of the old one isn't at hand?'

'It's here in the drawer,' said Kildare, pulling one open. 'These cards don't go into the files.'

He had it out.

'Ah, it's you, at last, is it?' cried Gillespie. 'Give me the card. Isn't it almost time for the injection, Jimmy?'

The weariness of the old man was so great that his head wavered a little from side to side as he spoke. He was trying to keep up his strength with the heat of his own temper and having a bad time of it. An ugly blue tint was in his face. His lips were a dull purple. Kildare's frightened eyes took heed of these details.

'It's not time for the injection,' said Kildare. 'The time has gone by. It's three hours too late. I warned you before I left, sir.'

'Did you? Did you warn me about them?' said Gillespie, his head falling back against the top of the wheel chair and his eyes closing. 'This infernal brain of mine is full of fuzz and won't work . . . How long will it take us to bring another batch of them around to the same point?'

'Four days, sir,' said Kildare.

'Four days? Four days lost?' echoed Gillespie. 'Then let's get at it at once—but my God, the pity of it, Jimmy! Why weren't you here with me, boy? . . . Four beautiful days lost . . .'

He had not opened his eyes as he spoke, and now his head fell suddenly over toward his shoulder. Kildare did not have to pause to take a pulse or make the slightest further examination. He knew every detail of that rugged face with such a perfect intimacy that the slightest alteration was diagnostic to him.

He called to Mary for adrenalin and pushed

the wheel chair into the next room toward the couch. Molly Cavendish hurried to Gillespie in silence. She did not need explanations or orders. Her eyes were deadly with hatred and accusation as she looked from her great master to Kildare. Then she was gathering up the loose body at the knees while Kildare lifted the torso. They laid him flat on the couch. Every moment the blue shadow deepened in his face as the life drained away. No one spoke. The nurses, with a windy whispering of their skirts, moved about him to anticipate his orders. Molly brought the alcohol to cleanse a spot for the needle; Mary Lamont offered the hypodermic syringe.

Kildare made the injection. Then with his eyes on the face of Gillespie and his finger on the pulse, he waited, counting the weak, shallow inhalations of breath and the senseless flutter of the heartbeat. Mary Lamont had opened the window. The entering wind caught at a loose paper on the desk so that it started rattling with the vibration of a snare-drum in the distance. A second injection was prepared in the syringe, but Kildare reserved it. Life was as dim in Gillespie as a fish motionless against a muddy stream.

Over the rattling of the paper on the desk he heard Mary Lamont whisper: 'Will he live, Molly? He's *got* to live!'

The more audible murmur of the older nurse answered: 'It don't matter. The leech that sucks the life out of him will still be working.'

'Hush, Molly!'

'*He'll* be as hushed as a stone before many days.'

The whispers died out, but the words kept on living in Kildare. He resaw the story of his days with Gillespie, and the truth of Molly's accusation yawned at him like a cannon's mouth. It was he who drew out the strength from Gillespie—he and the experiment.

The blue in Gillespie's face was altering now to gray. A vague flush of life commenced to shine again faintly, like dawn through a heavy fog. The respirations grew deeper; some order came into the riot of the heart. Kildare held the cold, bony hand of the old man, and in that quiet moment as he waited he made his resolution. It meant so much that the spirit sickened in him, as though part of his life were passing from his body back into that of Gillespie.

'Four days...' said Gillespie, without opening his eyes.

'We'll make them up,' answered Kildare.

'We've got to hurry,' said Gillespie. 'We're behind... Jimmy—take care—everything.' A moment later his gray lips parted in deeper breathing as he slept. Kildare, with a stethoscope, listened for a long time to the fluctuating, uncertain heartbeat, a foolish engine for a ship of such importance.

He stood up and found one leg numb from

kneeling so long beside the couch. Mary Lamont smiled at him as though he had brought back the dead to life, but old Molly Cavendish scowled down at the sleeper and gave Kildare not a single glance. The Cavendish was right. Now he kept asking himself if Gillespie would attempt to carry on the experiment single-handed if Kildare left him, or if he would abandon the whole enterprise.

He had to be alone to think things out, so he went back to his room, but found Collins sprawling there as usual. He turned to go out again.

'Wait a minute,' called Collins.

Wearily Kildare faced him.

'What's wrong?' asked Collins. 'Who's got a knife in you now?'

'Shut up, Tom,' said Kildare. 'Everything is all right.'

'Not by the look of you. You take everything the hard way. Want to be alone here?'

'It doesn't matter,' said Kildare. 'I keep hoping that I haven't made up my mind, but I suppose I have.'

'Made up your mind to what? You need a transfusion,' said Collins. 'You need a shot of happy blood without so many red corpuscles in it. Why not do things the easy way for once in your life?'

'The easy way?' said Kildare. 'That's right. That's what I'm going to do—right now.' He managed to laugh a little.

'You sound like the ghost in "Hamlet,"' stated Collins. 'Tell me what's wrong.'

But Kildare was gone. He went up to Carew and was able to see him at once.

'I've changed my mind,' said Kildare. 'I'll take the Messenger case.'

Carew, to his surprise, showed more curiosity than pleasure.

'Not because I tempted you, I hope. You've got permission from Gillespie to take time off?' he asked.

'No,' said Kildare.

'You realize that it may mean a complete break between you and the great man?'

'I realize that.'

Carew, pursing his lips, looked into his own thoughts. 'I suppose I understand,' he said. 'You got a taste of comfort and soft living in the Messenger house and after that the hospital regime looked as long and dry as a desert. And yet you know, Kildare, that there is always that long chance—Gillespie *might* make a great man of you. You're going to risk that?'

'It seems that I am,' answered Kildare dryly.

'Ah?' murmured Carew. 'Well, Gillespie's hope about you goes where most dreams go—into the garbage can or out the window into the gutter ... I'll get in touch with Messenger at once. He'll be very pleased, I dare say ... And after all, this may turn out to be a great thing for the hospital—a great thing for your own future. I'm almost glad that you've turned out to be a practical fellow, Kildare.'

He picked up the telephone as he spoke, turning his head quickly away. Even Carew despised him for his decision. And when the news of it went abroad, what would the others say who had watched with envy and astonishment as Kildare climbed by the hard, straight road toward the top of the medical ladder? But facing them was nothing compared with telling Gillespie.

Half an hour later he was bewildered to find that the old man was already back in his wheel chair, intent upon the entangled problems of his experiment, shouting orders once more at Mary Lamont. 'Can't I turn my back, can't I blink my eyes and lie down for a moment without having you slip out of my sight?' he exclaimed when he saw Kildare. 'Lamont, get some more Petri dishes and put the agar in them.'

'I'd like to speak to you alone for a moment,' said Kildare.

'Don't be secretive, Jimmy,' advised Gillespie. 'There's mighty little reason for whispering in this world, and when you get to my age you'll understand it . . . But go on and leave us alone, Lamont.'

She already was out of the room.

'If you're going to talk about the little dizzy spell I had,' said Gillespie, 'I won't hear a word of it.'

'It's not that. It's other things that will go wrong with you,' replied Kildare. 'You've only a certain amount of strength, and it can't be replenished in you as it can in younger people.'

Gillespie made a brutally terse summing-up. He said: 'I'll do the addition for you. I'm old. There's a melanoma eating my body away. I have only a few months to live. And I ought to conserve the oil in the lamp so that it will cast a light as long as possible. Right?'

'That's my idea, sir,' agreed Kildare.

'You're wrong then,' exclaimed Gillespie. 'If there's something worth burning for, let all the oil be consumed to make one big flash. It might be a signal that will be seen across a whole ocean of time. If you look back through the centuries, Jimmy, you can't see the little dim souls that keep falling into oblivion like leaves from trees. You can see only the creatures that burned as they lived; you see them by their own light, and time can't exhaust it. It's like the difference between peace and war. In peacetime little happens. In war the trained soldier goes out with his life in his hand and throws it away like a gambling fool. One in a million receives glory in exchange. And we're soldiers in a war, Jimmy. The enemy is ignorance. Ignorance is the dark. And any man who can throw a light is a fool if he's not willing to die to do it. So we're going to rush on with the experiment. What if I pass out while I'm working? The great attempt is nine-tenths of accomplishment. And if I'm a bit reckless with the little I have left to spend, why, I always have that young Doctor Kildare to complete what I've started.'

He laughed aloud and struck his hands together.

'They can beat us one by one, Jimmy, but they can't beat us when we hold fast together.'

The thing had to be said, and Kildare said it slowly. The words had a strange taste in his throat.

'The point is that I won't be here—at least for a time. I've told Doctor Carew that he can assign me out on the Messenger case...'

'You've told him what? You've told him what?' shouted Gillespie. 'What sort of infernal nonsense is this anyway? You know perfectly well that I can't have you assigned out when we're in the middle of the experiment. I'd as soon have no assistant at all as a will-o'-the-wisp who's here today and gone tomorrow and never to be counted on!'

'I'm sorry,' answered Kildare.

'To the devil with your sorrow!' cried Gillespie. His voice changed to a quieter tone that took the breath out of Kildare. 'It's not possible that you're thinking of walking out on me!'

Kildare looked away from his old preceptor and through the window toward the rain that slanted down in a fine sweep of brilliance borrowed from the shining west. In comparison, the interior of the office was lost in a twilight. So are all our hours and our days until some touch of genius lights them. He remembered what Gillespie had said of the dim souls who are lost by millions in the fog of time. He would be one of them, no doubt, if he lost his opportunity of borrowing light from this great man.

But he found himself repeating the lesson of Carew: 'It seems to me that a man ought to have a chance to live—I mean, I'd like to get some taste out of life before I'm an old man.'

'I don't believe it!' exclaimed Gillespie.

'It's true,' lied Kildare. 'From the time I was a small youngster, I've had a tough time of it. Now I see my way clear to get into the long green and I want some of it.'

'Are you drunk?' demanded Gillespie harshly.

'No, sir. I'm simply seeing some of the realities. I'm just a little tired of the life I've been leading.'

'Am I a fool?' barked Gillespie.

'Certainly not, sir.'

'Did I pick you out as my assistant?'

'Yes, sir.'

'After twenty-five years of searching to find some brain that might be worth the teaching I could give it, did I select you from all the thousands?'

'It was a great honor,' said Kildare.

'And now, after I've tried you and tested you

and hammered you for flaws and tested you with acids and found you the true metal—after all these tests, do you dare to tell me that I'm wrong? Do you have the impertinence to suggest that I've taken, not a thoroughbred who loves the hard going, but a cold-blooded, common rascal who prefers to have his beer and beef like a swine at a trough?'

Kildare was silent. A weight he could not support was bending his head. He wanted to shout out suddenly that nothing but Gillespie's own good was a strong enough force to take him from the old man's side and their work, but he knew that this would merely be temporizing. If it came to talk of such expedients, the clever Gillespie would be much too sharp for him. The break he was determined to make had to be accomplished with a knife-stroke, and the edge he used necessarily must be sharp.

'Around us in this room,' said Gillespie, extending his hands with a certain nobility, as though he were picking up the sorrows of the world and accepting the burden, 'there are the elements of a specific cure for which tens of thousands, hundreds of thousands, millions of people eventually may thank James Kildare and Leonard Gillespie. They may owe their lives to us.'

His voice changed wonderfully as he added: 'Jimmy, Jimmy, I know that you're young, and I know that all youth is tempted. But in the pinches, lean on me, talk to me. I can help you through the hard times.'

Kildare could not lift his head. He could not speak. Gillespie said suddenly: 'Then get out and stay out!'

Kildare got out, still dumb as a beast that has been kicked from a place where it is not wanted. Through a blur of pain he saw Mary Lamont looking at him with bewilderment and then with a queer alarm. A moment later the ring of Gillespie summoned her, and she went hastily in to the old man.

He lay far back in his chair with his head sunk on his chest.

He said at once, rather faintly: 'Be easy. I'm not going to faint twice in one day. Damned indigestion and nothing else. You understand?'

'Yes, doctor.'

'Come over here where I can see you with the light in your face. That's better. Lamont, you look like a pretty clean piece of goods to me. No lies and deceits in you, are there?'

She was silent. Her troubled eyes dwelt on him with infinitely gentle consideration.

'No lies and deceits even for the sake of that same young doctor for whom you keep your special look? Do you know what your special look is like, Lamont?'

'No, sir,' she said. Then: 'Will you lie down, doctor? Your color is not very—very good.'

'Isn't it? But I'm well enough, I'm so well

that I could chew up tenpenny nails or drink molten lead. That's how well I am. I think it's very possible that I may have made a fool of myself about a person who's important to me. I may have wasted—not time—ah, that doesn't count!—but life, life, life! I may have wasted that. And to be a fool—to call yourself a fool—is to send yourself living into hell and to burn ... Tell me, Lamont—do you love Kildare?'

'I think I do,' she said.

'Are you such a child that you're not sure?'

'I'm not a child,' she answered. 'But I'm not sure.'

'Because the blockhead, the blind man, keeps on treating you like a sister?'

She smiled for Gillespie again with enough pain in her eyes to keep him from pursuing the subject.

'However, if you love him, it means that you know him. He has opened his mind and his heart even without knowing it, if you love him. Tell me, then: Is it possible that our young Kildare, the fellow without fear, the man who hangs onto his purposes like a bulldog—is it possible that our young Kildare is a fellow who would give up the great chance of his life for the sake of money and an easy berth?'

'Give up?' breathed the girl. 'Give up this? Give up *you*? He never could do it! But...'

A memory stopped her.

'But... you'd forgotten what he said or did

on a certain day. And when you remember that, you're not so sure about his blind devotion. Is that correct? Lamont—tell me in a word! Could he do it?'

She did not answer, for the memory of how Kildare had groaned under the rub of privation in the hospital began to grow larger and larger in her mind's eye. She had the look of one who sees calamity approaching on wings and about to strike.

'He could,' said the old man softly. 'He could sell his soul for the damned, damned mess of pottage. That's what you haven't the heart to tell me.'

There was enough grief in her to have brought tears to another woman, but she kept looking, dry-eyed, at her new conception of the man she loved. Gillespie, putting an arm around her, drew her close to his wheel chair. He was about to say something that might act as a small comfort to her, but the words stuck suddenly in his throat so that for a moment the two of them were silent, looking into emptiness and seeing the same image.

Kildare, back in his room, packed the necessary clothes in one suitcase and, when he finished, there was very little left in his closet. If he put together in a heap all his possessions in the world, a single trunk, and a small one at that, would hold them all. A few years from now, if he followed the way that was opening before him, this would not be true. He would have his automobile, his country club for golf and tennis, his fishing tackle and guns, his clothes for all occasions. Instead of a drunken ambulance driver, a bartender, Mary Lamont and the great Gillespie, he would have a thousand acquaintances; he would have a ready smile, a warm handshake, and a fat-faced emptiness of mind.

In a crisis most men soften, but a few turn grim. Kildare was as hard as a rock when he stared out of the hospital, yet an uncontrollable force diverted him to the Gillespie offices before he left. When he found out that the internist was in another part of the hospital, he went straight to the inner office which was being used as their laboratory. Mary Lamont was there, tidying up with busy hands. She looked at him with a sudden flash of expectancy.

'Doctor Gillespie is gone, but only for a moment. He'll be right back,' she said.

'I don't need to see him,' said Kildare. 'And perhaps you can find something to do in the front office?'

'Yes, doctor,' she said. The bright hope had gone from her. Leaving the room, her head was bent to that angle which we hope will hide the tears in our eyes. Kildare was left alone looking out the window at the blue dusk with the rain streaking down through it and rattling softly on the glass like the noise of far-off drums. The metaphor grew in his mind. All the honest men of the world were continually marching to battle, but he was giving up the fight.

He realized that he had come to the laboratory with no definite purpose, but found himself a moment later with a cage of the white mice in his hands. Their bright little eyes twinkled up at him through the shadow. They were most obscure moments of existence, these tiny creatures, but considering the purpose they were serving here, they were to Kildare as important as the stars in the sky. The pain became so great in him that his head pulled back and his eyes closed. All hope of the shining glory was shut away from him forever.

CHAPTER TEN

Charles Herron had simple beliefs, and not many of them. He was moved by a deep loyalty to his family, his friends, his college, his country. People who have faith in a cause can give themselves to it with a calm deliberation, and Herron, because he did not examine comparative values, fought as hard for his football team as he would have fought for his country. As a lawyer he was worthless unless he trusted in the innocence of his client, but when he had faith in the justice of his cause, his solemn conviction warped judges to his side and was irresistible before a jury. He maintained about his life a wall which excluded the outer world, but those who managed to pass the gate were lords of all they surveyed. A nation composed of men like Herron would be given utterly to the pursuits of peace, but would be an overwhelming force in time of war. His faults were all of the mind and none of the heart. His interests were not many because he took nothing lightly. His touch was somewhat heavy because at times he lacked that ultimate and qualifying grace, a sense of humor. He insisted on putting all of his cards face up on the table, and he could not realize that most men and all women have only a vague interest in the truth. In Athens he would have been considered a blockhead; in Rome he would have been one of the first men of the state.

When he found Nancy Messenger stretched on a couch in her father's library, it did not occur to Herron to look at her twice before he opened his mind; in fact he considered it treason to withhold his innermost thoughts from the people concerned. By way of preamble he merely said: 'It's a surprise to find you here. I didn't know that you liked this room.'

'I don't,' said Nancy, 'but I like the sun that's shining into it just now.'

He observed, in fact, that the autumn sun was pouring upon her so that her white wrap dazzled his eyes. It was a very soft wool, a fluff of light weaving that shone like a cloud in the sky. Herron came around beside her. His huge shadow at once shut away two-thirds of the sunlight that had been streaming over her.

'That's one of the things I wanted to ask you about,' he said. 'I mean, there's this queer passion you have for the sun lately.'

'Don't ask me about it, Charles,' she said, her weary eyes closing. 'Everything that lives wants the sun.'

'Perhaps you were made for it,' answered Herron. 'There's something about you that shines, Nancy, and yet a shadow can come over it. That's what I worry about a little. Just now I wish I had you in a gay place like Paris.'

'Paris isn't gay,' said Nancy.

'Really?'

'No. On the boulevards think of those horrible kiosks covered with advertisements.'

'So Paris isn't gay? Let's think about that for a moment.'

'Oh, but I wish I were there, though. Every English-speaking city is so horribly dull.'

'Why so dull, my dear?'

'Because they speak so much English in them,' said Nancy, with classical logic. 'And then in Paris the day never ends. Life goes on there like a river to the sea. But over here everything is artificial. We have electric clocks to keep our consciences on edge. They tell us when to go to bed. Alarm clocks get us up in the morning. Everything is broken and chopped up. There's no continuity. It's like rehearsing life and death every day. The whole world wakes up and buzzes and pretends to be alive; and then the whole world lies down and closes its eyes and is really dead!'

She gripped her hands together hard.

'You know, Nancy, you're a little nervous,' said Herron. 'I think that a trip would be good for you.'

'Away from home? No, no!' She shuddered at the thought of leaving.

'That's queer,' said Herron. 'I thought you'd like to get away.'

'Please don't!' broke in Nancy. 'Please don't talk, darling.'

He was, accordingly, perfectly silent, telling himself that women are not as men. Torn between the strength of logic and the strength of faith, there was something rather naive and childish about the lawyer. Perhaps a chief reason for the girl's love of him was her understanding of his need of her. In the middle of this thoughtful silence she startled him by saying: 'Charles!'

'Yes, dear?'

'Don't leave me.'

'Of course I won't—until I have to go back to the office.'

'Don't go to the office. Don't ever go back to it.'

The absurdity of life without an office pleased a rare funny bone in Herron, and he laughed a little. As he laughed, he was loving Nancy more than ever.

'Tell me something,' said Nancy.

'Certainly,' said Herron. 'What is it?'

'Oh, do I have to put the words in your mouth every time?'

'But, Nancy, of course I love you.'

'Forever?'

'Forever.'

'No, only until it comes time for you to go to sleep again, and then you forget as thoroughly as though you were dead.'

'You're a bit nervous,' said Herron, suddenly at sea and afraid of this trend of talk. 'Just now you're *very* nervous, Nancy. And that leads me back to the idea of home.'

'I hate ideas,' said Nancy.

'You don't mean that,' said Herron softly. 'But the fact is that you've been spending so little time at home that I wonder if you care much about it.'

'Don't, Charles.'

'I've hurt you and I'm sorry. But isn't it obvious that you're needing a change? That's why I'm suggesting that we take a trip together.'

'*We*?' echoed Nancy. 'Together?'

'Why not?'

'Ah, that would be heavenly,' said Nancy.

'Would it? Then we can be married right away.'

'No, no!' cried Nancy.

'Do you say "no"? Let me try to see what's in your mind when you say that.'

'Thank God you can't see what's in my ugly, ugly mind.'

'Ugly? It's the only perfect thing I know! Nancy, what's the matter? Two weeks ago you liked talking about our marriage. It was to be as soon as I could arrange for a little time off. Well, I've arranged it now. We could get married tomorrow if you . . .'

'No—please!—Charles, I love you!'

This perfect *non sequitur* struck Herron dumb. It appeared that Nancy loved him, and therefore she would not talk of marrying him! He had a sudden desire to be alone in his office among his books; but then he realized with a sudden shock that though he might search through all the books of wisdom in the law or outside of it, he never could find in print an explanation of Nancy Messenger. He was almost glad of an interruption, for here the door of the room opened and Paul Messenger came in with that new guest of the house, John Stevens, that rather pale and withdrawing young man who nevertheless, it appeared, had been tireless in his all-night excursion with Nancy. As the two men entered the room, John Stevens was speaking to Messenger, and at the sound of his voice Nancy opened her eyes and cried out happily. She was on her feet at once and hurrying across the room with both hands held out. She cried: 'Johnny, Johnny, Johnny, I thought you'd left us forever!'

Herron never had seen her pour herself out on a man as she did on this comparative stranger. Stevens accepted the warmth of that greeting as though it were the most casual thing in the world. The embarrassed eye of Herron turned to Paul Messenger, but found him looking upon the pair and their greeting with an eye of unfathomable approval.

A moment before there had seemed in Nancy hardly strength enough to hold open her eyes; now she was happy, as busy, as gay as a singing bird. Presently she had her John Stevens in a chair by the window and was sitting opposite him with an air of delighted possession and triumph.

It was easy, shielded by the happy chatter of Nancy, for Herron to find sufficient privacy to say to Messenger: 'Long-lost cousin—or something like that, isn't he? Who *is* this Stevens fellow?'

'One of the best chaps in the world,' said Messenger reassuringly.

'Nancy seems to have no doubt about it,' answered Herron, frowning.

'Don't take the wrong tack,' cautioned Messenger. 'Absolutely the most trustworthy lad in the world.'

'It's pretty clear that Nancy would agree to that,' commented Herron. 'Well, I'll have to get back to the office. I want to talk with you, though.'

'Of course. Any time,' said Messenger. 'Nancy, Charles has to go along.'

'Does he?' she said indifferently, but then as though realization came to her at second hand, she rose from her chair and went across the room to her fiancé. 'I'll go down to the door with you, Charles,' she said. And at the door she turned to call over her shoulder, 'But I'm coming straight back, John!'

CHAPTER ELEVEN

'She likes you—an amazing lot, considering she's known you such a short time. One would have thought, when she went out with Herron just now, that she was leaving the best part of her thoughts behind her, with you,' commented Messenger. 'You know, you haven't told me how you managed to grow so close to Nancy.'

'I let her think that I have her own trouble—the same insomnia and the fear of the night. So now she wants to help me.'

'Ah, you have the devising mind that breaks down barriers and seems to make the whole world kin,' commented Messenger, 'but I suppose that you know women. All the young fellows today do.'

Kildare looked steadily at him.

'You're a little troubled,' he said at last, with

his own peculiar species of frankness, 'because I'm to spend a good deal of time with Nancy.'

'Not at all,' said Messenger, making a gesture that dismissed the suggestion.

Kildare shook his head. He insisted: 'You feel that manners come out of breeding, and breeding must be old and good. You're an old family. I suppose that there was a Messenger with the Conqueror. Herron is an old family too, so he's all right with Nancy, but you'd like to know more about me, wouldn't you?'

'There's a hint of truth in what you say,' answered Messenger, 'but not enough to make *me* say it. All of us are filled with prejudices, you'll admit, but as long as we *know* they're prejudices, they don't poison us. As for you, Kildare, I've heard enough from the Chanlers . . .'

'I'm the son of a poor country doctor,' said Kildare. 'Somewhere our name goes back to a village in Limerick County in Ireland. We're not predominantly Irish, though. If we were, I'd be enough proud of it, but we're a hodgepodge of Irish and English and German and Scotch; there was an Italian greatgrandmother somewhere; a French strain is in the blood too; and I think there was a dash of Russian not so far back. So you see, I'm nothing in particular. My father is a very simple fellow; my mother is just the same sort. We're lower middle class. We don't know any fine people. Most of our friends don't keep a servant. None of us have traveled a step. People with big names embarrass us a little. They make us feel all thumbs and stupid, as though they were laughing at us. I'm so far from the things you put a lot of value on that I don't even feel the worth of them. I wouldn't ask for a famous old name because I wouldn't know how to wear one.'

He finished this long, quiet speech with a smile, but Messenger was very solemn in his answer. He said: 'Most of us have scrambled blood lines. Once that would have been considered a pity perhaps. But today we say people have cold blood or are thoroughbred, according to their performance. Shall we let it go at that?'

There was nothing to do but let it go at that, yet Kildare was left with a strange sense of having stepped out and found no floor beneath his feet. He had extemporized a diagnosis of Paul Messenger's state of mind and found with something of a shock that he actually had struck the bedrock of truth. So far as the rich man was concerned, Kildare was a sort of scientific servant of the house, an annoying necessity, and to be trusted perforce because there was no other way to use him. He could understand now the magnificent insouciance of Messenger and the calmness of his trust that, granted good blood to begin with, money would solve all the problems of life. It was simply that he considered the rest of the world an infinite step beneath him and his peers. To Kildare a man was what he seemed to be, and a good fellow until he was proved otherwise by the course of events; to Messenger, the study of several vanished generations was necessary first, and without that information about a man's background he never would be able to know him with satisfactory surety. It sickened Kildare a little and gave him a preoccupation that remained in his mind until that night. Then he rang the hospital. He tried the nurses' home for Mary Lamont and her pleasant voice came back to him over the wire.

'I feel as though I'd been a long time away,' said Kildare. 'Will you tell me what's going on?'

'Doctor Gillespie is gone!' she said. 'He's gone away. He's left us.'

'Wait a minute,' said Kildare. 'Gone? Gone where?'

'Somewhere in Staten Island to be alone—and forget the hospital.'

'And given up the experiment?'

'He couldn't carry it on alone,' she said.

He felt a melancholy sense of triumph in that; for if he had sacrificed himself and thrown away the thing that was nearest his heart, at least he had accomplished his purpose. Gillespie would rest and come back refreshed.

'And you?' asked Kildare.

'I'm back on general duty,' she answered.

'I'm sorry about that.'

'Oh, don't think of me. It's Doctor Gillespie . . .'

'He was furious with me, wasn't he—a shouting fury, I suppose?'

'He was as still as a stone.'

'That's not possible,' said Kildare.

'I think his heart is broken,' she said, her voice trembling. 'And good-by, Doctor Kildare.'

She rang off on him suddenly and left him in a continuing daze. If Mary Lamont treated him in this manner, he could guess the general state of mind in the hospital. In their eyes, no doubt, he had sold his soul for a mess of pottage. As he thought of that, he wished that he never had laid eyes on Nancy Messenger or heard a syllable of her problem, but the malice went out of him when they were face to face again, for she looked to him with a confident, disarming eagerness.

'Let's not go near the sort of people we were with last night,' she said. 'They kill time, but they leave it dead. Let's go out and just ramble until we find a place to eat—and then follow our noses.'

She seemed to take it for granted that every night would be theirs together.

So they went out, not with a chauffeur, but in Nancy's two-seater convertible coupé. She preferred to drive it herself, and tooled it swiftly and smoothly through the traffic.

'I like to drive in a crowd like this,' said

Nancy, 'because you can take a few corners and twist through the traffic so that unhappiness gets in a tangle and loses sight of you and then never catches up for hours and hours. Isn't that true?'

'Of course it's true,' said Kildare. 'We may leave it behind so far that it'll never catch up at all.'

'*You* could leave it that far behind,' she agreed. 'There's nothing that forces it back on *you*, Johnny.'

He thought it might be the best of all opportunities to put the crucial question to her at a moment like this, when the driving of the car took most of her mind.

So he said: 'What is it that forces the unhappiness on you, Nancy?'

The car swerved a bit as her nerves jumped.

'Don't ask me; never ask me!' she said.

'I mean, it's not something that you can sleep away?'

'Never!'

'And it can come over you night or day?'

'Oh, Johnny, only a thought of it and I'm ready to die! Don't let me talk about it.'

'Talking is the only thing that does us any good, isn't it?'

'It helps you, but it never could help *me* for long.'

He was silent, trying to fit this last strange news in with the rest of his picture of her.

She changed the subject at once, saying

'What have you done to father? Usually a man is under the microscope for a long time before he's accepted as you've been.'

'He has a good instinct. He sees that I'm harmless,' said Kildare.

'But his whole attitude is rather odd. It's almost as though he *needed* you!'

He was glad when she let that topic drop, in turn, and went on to something else.

They had left the thicker traffic, in the meanwhile, but he was blind to where they were going, lost in his problem. He was only aware of the summery warmth of the air, a strange Indian summer mildness that had melted the ice away and dried the pavements and left a soft languor in the blood. He was half aroused when she brought the car up to the curb.

'Here we are,' she said. 'Here's a place that I've heard about. No one that we know is apt to be here, and we can talk, Johnny, and do a whole ocean of forgetting.'

There was an odd touch of familiarity about the scene, as though he had at least noticed a picture of it somewhere, but his mind was not clear at all until they walked down steps from the street under a sign that said 'Cesare's Restaurant.' He remembered well enough then. He had seen Cesare's scrawny little daughter, Francesca, through a bad attack of scarlet fever, and he had watched her with such care that Cesare and his wife felt he had given their girl back to them from the dead. The restaurant, in fact, was not six blocks from the hospital. They were in the very center of Hell's Kitchen where anyone on the street might recognize him at any moment. He was 'doc' to the whole district, and one single use of that nickname would expose him and identify him in the eyes of Nancy, who dreaded and hated all doctors. He would be revealed as a spy. The shock was so complete and unexpected that he could not bring to his lips a single word of protest before they were in the place and it was too late to turn the girl about.

It was far, far too late, for a big form turned from the bar at this moment and he saw Weyman, the ambulance driver, wave a great arm of recognition above his head, shouting, 'Hi...'

Kildare, looking at him without a flicker of recognition, closed his left eye and kept it closed for an instant. Weyman dropped his arm. The joy melted from his face in separate chunks, leaving the features in an odd disarray.

'Sorry. Took you for somebody else,' said Weyman, turning abruptly away. 'Another shot, bartender,' he ordered.

A waiter was taking Kildare and the girl to a corner table.

'Poor fellow,' said Nancy. 'The man at the bar thought for a moment that you were an *old* friend, didn't he?'

'Old friend' Weyman had at that moment

stopped Cesare as he swept in to greet the new customers. On the Italian's face appeared first a momentary fog of bewilderment, then a grin of understanding so profound that it wrinkled the stiff red varnish of high health that covered his cheekbones. He turned, disappeared into the kitchen, and presently came magnificently into the dining room again. Kildare could rest assured that the wife and the daughter had been well warned against recognizing their doctor in that interval. In fact Cesare, as he bowed by the table and pointed out his recommendations for the evening, had eyes only for the 'signorina'; he gave not so much as a trailing side glance to Kildare. Yonder was the tall, awkward bulk of Weyman taking another newcomer by the shoulder and dragging him up to the bar for a drink. A fine perspiration turned the face of Kildare cold as he recognized young Nick himself, who might have burned up Salt Creek had it not been for the 'doc'; but neither Nick nor Weyman turned even for a fleeting instant toward the intern.

There seemed no real hope that he could escape from this district without being hailed by some affectionate voice, maudlin with good feeling, but his heart was warmed by the tact of Weyman and the rest. He would not have dreamed of finding such a quick response from them.

He wanted to use this, which was probably his last moment with the girl, in some desperate effort to break through to her secret, that hidden cause of unhappiness from which, she seemed to think, escape was impossible; but she grew interested in the Neapolitan songs of that fat Caruso who sweated over his mandolin and sang for the pleasure of Cesare's customers, and between the music and the many courses there was no chance for continued conversation. The restaurant had filled every chair before they left. There were at least ten people whom he knew, but not an eye turned toward him as he took the girl out of the place at last.

As they stepped to the automobile at the curb, his sense of relief was like a fresh wind in his face, but Nancy was instantly pointing out a crowd which filled an adjoining block of the street near a settlement house. They had a blaring music of horns and drums and hundreds of people were dancing.

'There! There we are!' said Nancy. 'Come on, Johnny! Isn't it better than all the night clubs in the world?'

'You'll wear out your shoes—you'll drag yourself to death trying to get over the pavement,' protested Kildare.

'Oh, I can pick up my feet and make them step,' said Nancy, laughing, and Kildare went gloomily with her towards the excitement.

He had escaped recognition in the restaurant owing to the providential foresight of Weyman, but he could not escape it in the happy, cheerful, milling crowd that filled the street. A hundred people would know him. Weyman and Nick, stepping long and large, went past them, Weyman giving his arm a hard nudge as he moved by. He noticed that with a dull eye of trouble, and then he came with Nancy to the roped-off area.

Before him, vaguely, he saw Nick and Weyman separately accosting people, then lost in the mob as he stepped out in the dance with Nancy in his arms.

He had not taken ten steps with her when a twelve-year-old lad pointed a sudden arm at him and cried: 'Hey! Look at...'

His partner, a freckle-faced, scrawny little girl, slapped him suddenly across the mouth; they whirled away into the crowd.

'What in the world was the matter with that boy?' asked Nancy.

'He didn't like my dancing steps,' said Kildare. 'And his partner thought he was being rude. Wasn't that it?'

'No, I think they like the way you dance; or else they like *you*, Johnny,' said the girl. 'Every one of those children have a smile when we go past them.'

Half of them, in fact, were gaping and grinning at Kildare as he moved slowly on with Nancy, but not a word of greeting reached him, not a single voice hailed him by the nickname which they had learned to call him through the district. It came over him suddenly that the word of Nick and Weyman already had been passed from mouth to mouth through the entire throng—the 'doc' wished to walk invisible tonight, and they were willing to play the game for him with all their might. The older lads and girls grew elaborately unaware of him as he came near; the very children managed to keep their voices still even if they could not turn their eyes away. Nancy had her own interpretation.

'We amuse the children,' she said, 'but the grown-ups don't like us. They want to have their good time to themselves and to them we're intruders.'

'I think you're right. And we'd better go,' said Kildare.

'I wouldn't go for worlds,' she answered. 'There's something queer about the way they treat us, and I want to find out what it is. A lot of them simply fail to see us, for instance. We might as well be two ghosts, Johnny. Do you notice?'

'We don't belong. That may be it,' agreed Kildare.

But up and down that pavement he had to move with Nancy until a tag dance came. He was certain that no one would take Nancy from him but, after a moment, he saw Nick, with a set, rather desperate look on his handsome young face, come sidestepping through the crowd towards him, tapped Kildare, and instantly was gliding away with

Nancy. Kildare drifted back toward the rope.

The voice of Weyman growled behind him: 'She looks like one of the ones, doc. But whatcha mean bringing her over here where everybody knows you?'

'I didn't bring her. I was brought. Weyman—it means a great deal to me if I can get out of this without being spoken to. D'you think it's possible?'

'It's as good as done, doc,' said Weyman. 'Don't turn your head or maybe she'll see us talking . . . Is she a nifty or is she a nifty? . . . But you can walk all the way through Hell's Kitchen, now, and nobody'll see you. There ain't a cop on a beat that'll know your face. There ain't a stevedore down on the docks that'll be able to see you. There ain't a lunchwagon cook that ever laid eyes on you. Nobody ever heard of Doc Kildare before. We've put it on the underground wire and the whole damn district is wearing blinders. Here they come again with Nick steering her. Notice the dirty looks he's getting from some of the boys? They don't know that it's part of the game. Go ahead and get her, doc.'

Kildare went ahead and got her.

As Weyman had promised, Hell's Kitchen was blind to them, and before the night ended they had explored most of it. They went down by the docks where ships were being loaded by night crews and the lifts groaned and the pulleys rattled; they passed in and out of the little night clubs which fed beer and music to the young people of the district; they sat in all-night lunch wagons. Midnight had fallen well behind them and they had reached that hour of four in the morning when even New York grows quiet before Kildare saw commencing in the girl that fear which followed her in the night. Once more with empty eyes she began to consider some huge despair. That burden which invisibly crushed her was the weight which he had to find and transfer to his own hands. One vastly important surety was growing in him constantly: That which she feared was in herself, not in the outside world. Something like the sharp wound of conscience was consuming her.

After four in the morning she once or twice touched him and said: 'You're not too tired, Johnny? You still can keep going?'

'I was going to ask you the same thing,' he would answer, and then her smile came as a reward and a comfort: but he began to doubt his ability to continue in his own role of a man hounded by inward fear. One careless, unguarded moment of indifference might let her guess the truth and then he would be cast into outer darkness and all of his work with her would be undone. For in a case like this there was no real accomplishment except the final one. There was no question of coming by slow degrees to the ultimate answer. He had to wait for the revelation which might come at any instant. A single word, perhaps, would tell him everything. Such a great compassion grew in Kildare as he watched her that sometimes he almost forgot Gillespie and that wreckage of his hopes that lay behind him.

After six o'clock another idea came to Nancy Messenger.

She said: 'Johnny, when you're in a pinch, is it best to go find out the whole truth, no matter how bad it may be, or is it better to keep guessing—and hoping?'

'I'd rather find out the whole truth and look it in the eye,' said Kildare.

'Do you think you would?' she asked with a faint smile. 'Well—I'm going to try now. If there's an answer for me, it lies nearly two hours away in the country. Will you drive out with me? I'll take you to an old-fashioned breakfast; really golden biscuits and the only good coffee in the world.'

'Coffee!' said Kildare. 'That's what we want! And two hours right now are what we need to use up.'

In the car she gave up all pretense of cheerfulness. She slumped low in the seat with her head thrown back. She talked, as her habit often was, with her eyes closed and as they slid out over the great, gentle arc of the Fifty-ninth Street Bridge with Manhattan like shadowy, lifted hands behind them, she was saying: 'Was there something queer about tonight? Was it the people?'

'They were a good lot,' said Kildare. 'Beer is a bit easier to handle than champagne, you know.'

'Yes,' she agreed. 'They were cheerful and good-natured. But they made me feel like a ghost. Why was that?'

'They didn't look at you because you weren't their kind.'

'Oh, but there was that party in the second little night club—you remember?—those people who obviously were slumming? Everybody stared at *them*. They made fools of themselves patronizing and surprising the waiters with their orders. The crowd didn't like them and showed it.'

She considered this. Then he was aware that she was shaking her head slowly, dismissing this suggestion.

'They didn't look at us face to face, but they were terribly interested. Johnny, I never felt such a weight of eyes—from behind. There was something in the hiss of their whispering that was about me. A woman can always tell that sort of thing. I think they would have given a good deal to find out about us; and still they wouldn't look me in the face. The more I think about it, the stranger it was!'

'I didn't feel that way,' said Kildare.

After a moment she said: 'Did you ever see some important person traveling incognito?'

'No. Just what do you mean?'

'Well, I mean a prince or a king or the prime minister. If they're trying to be inconspicuous, well-bred people make the most desperate effort not to see them, and their eyes fairly ache with the effort of keeping them away from the prince. But all the time, of course, they're seeing nothing else. Well, it was like that tonight . . . Johnny!'

'Yes?'

'Are you somebody's double? I mean, do you look like some famous moving picture star or prize fighter or something like that?'

'I? Not that I know of.'

'You've never found that a crowd of people suddenly became awfully aware of you?'

'No. Never. Just the opposite. I'm the average man,' said Kildare. 'I'm the average height and the average mug and the average weight. I disappear into a crowd like sand in the sea.'

'Just the same, those people were terribly aware of you tonight. It's strange, isn't it? If they thought you were a celebrity, wouldn't they have come along and asked you to sign cards for them and all that embarrassing business?'

'What an idea!' said Kildare.

'Almost the strangest thing of all is that you didn't notice it because you have eyes that see everything.'

'I have? Aren't you imagining a few things tonight, Nancy?'

'Perhaps I am. I don't know ... Left, Johnny!'

Left he swung. They hit more open country at a higher speed. And as they rolled on among the fields, the sky gradually brightened around the horizon with the beginning of the day. But it seemed to give Nancy none of the pleasure and the reassurance which she had found in it the morning before. She grew more and more silent.

'Are you still thinking about the people in Hell's Kitchen?' he asked her at last.

'Thinking about them? No, no; I'd forgotten them a thousand years ago.'

What held her was the thing that lay ahead, then. Kildare tried to prepare himself for it. The daylight grew from a hint to a color and then to a brilliance that made the road lights dull. The sun was almost up when Nancy asked him to stop the car. He paused on the top of a low hill which looked down on a vague checkering of Long Island estates, their boundaries obscured by the trees. A narrow inlet from the sea wound back among the lowlands and joined a mere silver hint of a creek in the distance.

'That's what I used to know when I was a youngster,' said Nancy, sitting up. 'I mean, I used to be a part of all that. It was inside my skin and I was inside it. You know the way children can be?'

'I know,' said Kildare. 'When they're happy,

you mean?'

'I was the happiest girl in the world until I was—Well, it doesn't matter. But down in that inlet I learned to swim and sail and paddle a canoe and all that. The center of life was an old boathouse that's never used any more, I think. And we used to ride cross-country across those fields. And that white scar on the hill—you see?—every morning when I waked up, I looked at that through my window, over the tips of the trees on the edge of our place. From my window I saw this road also. It was the one that led toward the outside; it was the road to the city, where everything would be wonderful and life would be frightfully crowded and happy some day. You know?'

'Wouldn't you like to go back to those days?'

'And fall into this same trap? No, no, no!' said Nancy. And he felt her shuddering. 'I wouldn't want to live through a single day of it all if I knew what was coming in the end. Let's drive on. Nora will be awake by this time.'

He felt once more that he had come to the very verge of the mystery and again the door had been shut in his face, but a hope was quickening in him now. He was as guilty as a spy, but he guessed that he was on the verge of the great discovery.

Considering the almost fantastic wealth of Paul Messenger, the country place was extremely modest. It was high-shouldered, square-faced, and probably had plenty of room inside, but there was no show of elegance about it whatever. A profusion of the naked branches of climbing vines sprayed up its sides, and it needed freshening with white paint. In the near distance, an old red barn attended it. In fact, it looked more like a Southern farm than a suburban residence.

'There's smoke from the kitchen stove,' said Nancy, pointing, as the car rolled up the drive. 'Nora's up. John, for a while she was mother and father to me. She's ignorant and bad-tempered and positive and complacent, but she's also a dear. Will you try to remember that when we go in?'

It was hardly necessary for him to remember a thing, however, for no attention came to him, not even a glance. After Nora had seen her girl, she was too blinded by that vision to pay any heed to lesser things. She would not even let the guests stay in the living room, but carried Nancy straight out into the kitchen while she prepared breakfast. Kildare dawdled in the background with a smile of assumed sympathy but every sense on the alert to discover what he could. It was a foreign language of old association that the two women exchanged, but out of it he had to try to find some significant thread. If there were a secret in the air, he had high hopes that Nora never could conceal it. She was a big woman with a young, rosy face and white hair pulled back from her forehead so snugly that the horizontal wrinkles arched up into a constant query. She kept about her person, as about her kitchen, an atmosphere of hearty good-nature. The danger signal was in her pale blue eyes, which flashed every moment with variable lights. Perhaps she was fifty, but all her strength still was with her. When Kildare tried to help her carry into the kitchen a more comfortable chair for Nancy, she brushed him vigorously aside, using the chair for the gesture.

Nancy, leaning back in the comfort of her chair with her hands turned palm up on the broad arms of it, looked about her with half-closed eyes of contentment.

'Why do I see you so seldom, Nora?' she asked. 'Why are there such long times between?'

'Because I'm the only living thing in a dead house,' said Nora, adding fresh coffee and cold water to the big pot, 'and because youngsters are the great ones for forgetting.'

'Oh, but I never forget you; only it's a long way out here,' explained Nancy.

'Don't answer me back, but be still and let me look at you, darling,' said Nora.

'Ah, see there!' said Nancy, pointing. 'You've brought company into the old house at last.'

An old fox hound with his eyes abased by sorrowful wisdom and his ribs lean with age came limping into the kitchen through the porch door, trailing a forepaw. He begged permission with humble head and slowly wagging tail, then slunk to a pad by the stove and curled up on it. His attention followed Nora wherever she moved.

'It's not that I think any more of dogs than I ever did,' said Nora. 'The dirty things make a waste of cleaning in the house and a waste of time all through the lives of their masters.'

'You're forgetting Champion,' said Nancy.

'I'm forgetting nothing.'

'But you loved him.'

'I never did once, at all. But I loved the silly look of you when you were with him, was all. The great lout scattered his hair through the house and his stomach as uneasy as a weather-vane! But when I saw this poor devil skulking in the yard with his lame foot a week ago, I took him in, not because I wanted him here on my hands, but because I couldn't bear driving him away. I despise a beaten dog or a begging man, but I can't help putting my hand in my purse, Nancy, the more shame to me.'

She changed the subject by pointing suddenly to Kildare, as though she were inclined to include him among the beggars.

'What is this one now?' she demanded. 'You haven't been the grand young fool and thrown out big Charlie Herron, have you?'

'Hush, Nora. Of course not. But Johnny Stevens is a very dear friend of mine.'

'And that's all? Driving about with you in the middle of the night to the ends of the world?

Oh, hush yourself, Nancy, and don't try to be hushing me. There are two kinds of girls in the world: the one kind are the careful and the others are the fools. I'm going to roll out some biscuits for you, sweet.'

'I could eat them, Nora.'

'There was never a day when you couldn't and wouldn't,' said Nora. 'Ah, God, I remember the old times! You climbed and ran and fought—and lied—like a boy. And you were as hungry as your own mischief day and night.'

Kildare, entirely out of the conversation by this time, crossed the kitchen to the dog and began to examine the forepaw on which it would put no weight. The pad was soft and contracted as a sure sign that the limping had continued for some time. Nora, in the meantime, was mixing biscuit dough with the strong sure hands which make speedy work of every task. She was in the midst of chopping out the well-rolled layer into convenient circles for the baking pan when another thought made her dust her hands and rush out of the room, exclaiming: 'I almost clean forgot what I've been saving for you, darling. Wait here this minute.'

'She's a sweet old thing, isn't she?' asked Nancy.

'She needs a lot of knowing,' answered Kildare.

'Oh, but she'd die for the people she loves.'

'Maybe she would,' agreed Kildare, 'or kill them with kindness.'

'Now what do you mean by that?' asked Nancy, puzzled. But here Nora returned, beaming, and holding something with both hands against her breast.

'What do you think I have here?' she asked.

'An envelope full of old lavender.'

'Oh, it's something just twice as sweet.'

'I can't guess, Nora.'

'Where's your brain gone, then, if you can't guess more than once? Sweetheart, it's *her* picture when she was your own age and as like you as ever was—before even Paul Messenger came into her life, the poor lamb—before ever she was taken in by the dirty doctors that were the death of her in the end...'

Kildare looked sharply up at this. What he had just heard might open a thousand doors of his riddle. Nancy had taken the picture into her hands, but Kildare made sure that she gave it only the briefest glance. It seemed that whatever Nora found of beauty in it was all a blank for the girl. There must even have been something sharply distasteful, for she lowered the picture at once to her lap.

'Have I hurt you with it, Nancy dear?' asked the old nurse. 'How am I ever to know about you? The one minute you're as rough as a horse jumping fences and the next you're as tender as a kitten a week old and its eyes still blue with blindness. Give me back the picture, dear.'

'No, Nora. I want it. Of course I want it,' said Nancy, and yet Kildare could have sworn that she did not mean what she said.

Nora, having laid the rounds of biscuit-dough in the big baking pan, slammed home the door of the oven upon it.

'In twenty minutes we'll be at the table,' she said. 'Will you have coffee now, child?'

Here it was that Kildare's hand, abandoning the gingerly examination of the dog's paw, rose and began to fumble at his shoulder. The hound suddenly cried out on an almost human note of pain. Nora, whirling from the stove, exclaimed, with an accusing finger pointed: 'How did you find the pain was in the shoulder, young man? Are you a doctor, whatever?'

'Nora, don't be silly,' said Nancy.

'I was only petting the poor old fellow,' lied Kildare.

'Petting? It didn't have the look of petting. It had the look of questions you were asking with the tips of your fingers. You've found the seat of the pain and look if the poor old dog isn't trembling still! Nancy, your young John Stevens is a doctor or I was born a liar.'

'You were born a liar then,' said Nancy serenely. 'He's more apt to *need* a doctor than to be one.'

'Have it your own way,' growled Nora. She made some amends by saying: 'I'm sure there's no insult in asking a man if he's a doctor. Isn't most of the world proud to be one, after all?'

But Kildare felt that an arrow had whizzed close to his ear, and he could tell by the angry look of the nurse that a suspicion was still harbored in her mind.

CHAPTER TWELVE

They got through the breakfast happily enough with reminiscences of the old days which gave Kildare not an inch of ground to stand on during the talk. However, he had a chance to see the picture of Nancy's mother which Nora had just given to the girl. She looked as like Nancy as a sister, but she was made with a far greater refinement of feature. She lacked some of Nancy's expanse of forehead, but there was no sulky weight around her mouth; she had, instead, that radiant sweetness of face which seems to have gone out, in the very young, with the introduction of the one-piece bathing suit. Today the face is only one part of the familiar features. No matter how Kildare considered the picture he could not see the slightest reason for the manner in which Nancy had winced from the sight of it. Once more he felt, keenly, that he had found an arrow pointing forward to his goal, no matter how far away it might be.

The bright slant of the sun into the room made Nancy remember how the day was running on at last. She said: 'I'd almost forgotten that I have to talk to you alone, Nora...'

'If the doctor will wait for us here, then—' said Nora.

'I'll go outside into the sun,' answered Kildare, and left the house for the open air.

The mildness of the preceding evening still hung in the air. There was warmth enough to draw up a ground mist like that of spring, filling the hollows with a blue ghost of water and turning the horizon pale. The need for sleep grew suddenly in him; an ache fastened on the base of his brain and would not be rubbed away; but still he was satisfied, for in this old house he felt that he had come almost in touching distance of the solution of his mystery. That great mind of Gillespie's, looking with the inward and the outward eye, already would have come to a definite conclusion perhaps; but the mind of Gillespie was lost to him forever!

It seemed to Kildare, as that wretched aching extended through his heart, that he was shrinking almost physically into featureless obscurity. He had become a tiny object which the eye might lose entirely in a landscape like this. He had been growing like a tree. Now his tap-root was out. It was a sharp grief that left a pain in his throat, and the cry that he heard might almost have come from his own lips.

The sound of it made a great echo in his

brain, therefore, before he realized that it had come from the house. That wailing cry, high-pitched on a note of sorrow and horror, might have come either from the girl or the nurse. His impulse was to rush into the house. Perhaps the mystery was being bared at this very moment. He had to hold himself hard. The outcry had ended. The quiet of the morning gradually advanced about him with a hypocritical gentleness, again, but still his nerves were shuddering with the memory of that outcry from the house. It was too ugly to be given credence. An animal, unendurable pain had been in it, and yet something of the girl's voice was also in the sound.

He lighted a cigarette and began to walk up and down briskly. In spite of himself his step slowed and he found himself again standing beside the steps, looking at the brown grass, close-clipped between the stones of the old path. There had been almost too much life on this place, he was thinking, so that ancient trails and new were inextricably intermingled, the old patterns obscuring the fresh. After a moment his face grew cold with perspiration. He pulled out a handkerchief and scrubbed the moisture away. Then he heard the foot falls coming through the interior of the house.

The door, as it opened, showed him Nora on the threshold with her arm around the girl. He knew at once that it was Nancy who had felt the stroke of grief or of terror. She had been turned to a face of stone.

'I won't come down with you to the car, darling,' said Nora, in a weeping voice.

'No, Nora,' said the girl quietly.

'Ah, God, that *this* should come to us!' whispered the nurse.

'Hush, Nora.'

'I'll hush my mouth, but I can't hush my poor heart,' said Nora faintly. 'God keep you and bless you. Will you remember what I've said to you?'

'Yes,' said the girl, looking at the world with her empty eyes.

'You'll come again tomorrow?'

'Yes, I'll come.'

'Good-by then, my sweet lamb.'

'Good-by,' said Nancy. When she was half a step away, she turned again and kissed the wet face of Nora. Then she came smoothly down the steps with a smile prepared for Kildare. 'After all, it's pretty late,' she was saying. 'I suppose we ought to hurry back, Johnny?'

It was this smiling, it seemed to Kildare, that proved the infinite distance she had receded from him since he last was with her. She had been close enough for him almost to touch her thoughts, but now he was removed, as though by a strange language, far from everything that was in her mind. She could not see her own white look and for that reason, of course, she tried to deceive him with her smile and her quiet voice.

To explain the scene at the doorway she said, as they settled into the coupé: 'Poor Nora—some of them never learn control—at every little pain they break down. You've noticed that, Johnny, haven't you?'

He said: 'Don't talk, Nancy. I know you're sick to the heart. But don't make yourself talk.'

He felt her startled, straining eyes fixed upon him almost suspiciously as the car started and he ran through the gears.

He added: 'It's all right. I'm not going to ask any questions.'

'God bless you, Johnny,' she said.

She lay back against the cushion utterly spent.

'Nobody else,' she whispered. 'Nobody in the world would be like you about it—because none of the rest—none of them know what pain is, do they?'

He said nothing. He did not speak a word all the way back into the city, but drove along softly so that she could relax. She lay as though sleeping, always a white face bruised with purple around the eyes. Once the freshening pain in her mind brought a faint moan from her lips. Kildare, at that, put a steadying arm about her and she let her head lean against his shoulder. He drove on like that for a time, slowly, and when she sat up, he removed his arm without a word. So nothing was said between them all the way back to the city.

When they came into her father's house she

looked up at him with that faint, sick smile, saying good night. Kildare held her hand for a moment.

He said: 'Something's hit you pretty hard. I don't know what and I'm not asking you any questions. But if there's anything you want to do about it, will you let me try to help, Nancy?'

She read his face from left to right and back again, a great and calm affection in her eyes.

'There's nobody else in the world that I'd turn to,' she said.

He digested that speech and the connotations of it on his way upstairs; it meant that she would turn to him before she would to her father or to big Charles Herron.

It was a quarter to ten when he tapped on the door of Messenger. Messenger himself pulled the door open quickly and passed a hand over the troubled corrugations of his face as he saw Kildare.

'It's been a long night,' said Messenger. 'Come in!'

Kildare went in, looking rather vaguely about him.

'There's something to drink over there on the table,' said Messenger.

Kildare sniffed the pungency of good Scotch and poured out a stiff drink. It went down like water. He took another, lighted a cigarette, and sat down with it. All he could think about was the taste of the smoke and fire as the Scotch worked into him more deeply. A warm, friendly mist was forming across his brain.

'You're dead tired. You're dead,' said Messenger.

'I'm all right,' said Kildare.

'Can you tell me about Nancy?'

'Pretty soon. I know a little more. I want to ask you a few questions. A short time ago she sold her horse, didn't she?'

'Yes.'

'A fine mare she was very fond of—a good jumper and all that?'

'That's true.'

'What reason did she give?'

'It troubled me at the time very much,' said Messenger. 'I think she said that horses were all right, but that horsy people were a great bore. But it didn't ring true. That chestnut had been a great thing in her life.'

'You can't tell what suddenly made Nancy change her mind about riding?'

'No.'

'Has Nancy complained of bad health or pains?'

'Headaches. Otherwise, she's always been a tough, healthy specimen.'

'Along with the riding, she gave up every other form of exercise except dancing?'

'Exactly.'

'Because she was not physically fit?'

'I've never heard her say so.'

'Mr Messenger, will you tell me a little about Nancy's mother?'

Messenger said, after a moment, gently, as though he were granting his forgiveness to an intruder: 'Nancy's mother has been dead for ten years, Doctor Kildare.'

'That made Nancy about ten years old at the time. What were her relations with her mother?'

'Deeply, deeply affectionate,' said Messenger.

'No,' said Kildare.

Messenger lifted his eyebrows and waited. Kildare explained: 'I don't think so. Affectionate, perhaps; but there must have been something else.'

'Will you explain what you have in your mind?' asked Messenger.

'I have a thousand things in my mind,' said Kildare. 'I have to select something out of the thousand and try to concentrate on it. You'll help me, won't you?'

'You're upset,' said Messenger.

'I'm badly upset,' said Kildare.

He finished his drink and went over to the whisky bottle. There would be no hospital this day. He took that melancholy consolation to heart and then poured the third drink. He was beginning to taste the stuff now.

'Do you think that matters have come to a crisis?' asked Messenger. 'Is that what you mean?'

'I think they have decidedly,' said Kildare.

'If matters have come to a crisis,' persisted

Messenger, 'it means that Nancy is on the verge of some very important action.'

'Some very important action. Yes.'

'Something that might remind us of the Chanler case?'

Kildare thought back to that dreary room in the boarding house and the body of Barbara Chanler with the sheet drawn up over the face. A shudder began in the small of his back. He took a quick drink.

Instead of answering the question, he said: 'I don't want to discuss possibilities that may frighten you. I want to get information from you. Will you tell me a little about Nancy's mother?'

Messenger said: 'She was a very gentle person: brave, calm, and beautiful. I thought she was a perfect woman. I still think so.'

Kildare shook his head. Messenger said coldly: 'I assure you.'

'Between a character like that and Nancy nothing could have happened. It must be that you're not telling me everything. Was there any circumstance connected with the death of your wife?'

Messenger frowned at the floor.

'I'm a doctor,' said Kildare crisply. He thought of the pain that was in his own life and that would have to stay in it. He had to have the truth, even if it meant cutting with the knife. 'I have to have the truth, and the full truth,' he said.

The telephone rang. Messenger reached for it.

'I can't come just now,' he said into the instrument. 'Perhaps, in that case . . . Very well, I'll be right down.'

He put the telephone back in its cradle and stood up.

'Don't let anything stop us,' said Kildare. 'Let me have a chance to find out the facts.'

'It's impossible for me to tell them to you briefly,' said Messenger, 'and I have a call from my office that I can't avoid answering.'

Kildare followed him to the door of the room, saying rapidly: 'Is it possible that whatever you can tell me would have had any effect on Nancy?'

'I think it might,' said Messenger. 'Possibly it might. But ten years have gone by without a sign . . .'

'What's been buried even for thirty years sometimes works all the mischief,' said Kildare. 'When can you come back, or where can I see you?'

'I ought to be through in two or three hours. I'll come straight back here.'

'You can't make it faster than that?'

'I'll try to make it as brief as possible. Kildare—is Nancy very badly upset?'

'She's as badly upset as a human being can be,' said Kildare. 'Will you please stop asking me questions?'

The answer struck Messenger so hard that

he went out of the room without another word. Kildare followed out into the hall. As he stood there, he heard the descending feet of Messenger stumble twice on the stairs. The front door closed and the echo of its closing lived for a moment beside him in the upper room. After that, he threw off his clothes, walked through a shower, shaved, and dressed again. Then he dropped face down on the bed and fell into an instant sleep.

CHAPTER THIRTEEN

A noise picked at his brain like a woodpecker at a sensitive plant. After a while he was able to sit up and discover that the sound was a rapping at his door. He got to it and pulled it open on Nancy Messenger. She was dressed again for the street.

'I've had a call,' she said, 'and I have to go out. I wonder if you'll come, Johnny. Are you too dead?'

He stared at her.

'You can't go out again, Nancy,' he said. 'Don't go out, please.'

'I'm all right,' she said.

'You look rotten. You look all in,' said Kildare. 'Nancy, I'm terribly fond of you. Don't go out again. Try to rest a little, will you?'

'I can't,' she said, shaking her head, keeping her eyes hopelessly on him.

'Listen to me,' he said, 'you go and lie down on the library couch and I'll read aloud to you. I'm such a rotten reader that people always go to sleep in self-defense. You know?'

'Oh, Johnny, Johnny; it's no good,' she said. 'But where I'm going, maybe I'll find something that *can* help me.'

There was a possible double meaning in what she said that struck him cold.

'But I can't ask you to come along. You're too played out.'

'Nothing in the world could keep me from going along,' said Kildare.

He turned with her down the hall, down the stairs.

'Are we going to leave any word? About when we're coming back?' he asked her.

'It's no good getting them into bad habits,' she said, with a wan smile. 'They mustn't start expecting to know where I am. Because in the end—' She did not finish the speech.

They were in the front hall when she said this and the door was opened in front of them by Charles Herron. He put the key back into his pocket and took off his hat, still silently looking at her. Then he spoke gravely to Kildare and said to Nancy: 'You were hard to find last night, my dear.'

Kildare stepped away across the hall and turned his back on them as he pretended to look out the window on the formal little patch of garden at the rear of the house. He heard Nancy explaining: 'I was just following my nose and it led me to some unexpected places. That was all. Were you wanting me?'

Herron got his voice down a bit lower, but there was so much natural resonance that Kildare heard every word clearly.

'I telephoned to your friends. None of them had seen you. I dropped around to a dozen of the night spots which you seem to favor. You weren't around, and you hadn't been seen. I suppose you were with young Johnny Stevens?'

If the girl answered, Kildare could not hear the words.

Herron was saying: 'What is the mystery? Am I what makes you unhappy?'

'Don't go on,' said the faint voice of Nancy. 'Don't ask any more questions, Charles.'

'I spent the night hunting—and worrying. You were out till the morning and I was in hell. I know how fine you are, but I also know how rotten the night world is. You can't like it. Can you?'

'No. I don't like it.'

'Then what drives you to it? Is it because you want to get the thought of our marriage out of your mind?'

'No, Charles. No, please!' whispered the girl.

'Good God, Nancy, there's no use being pitiful about it. If you'll have me, I'm yours for the taking, and forever. I feel as though I was taking my life in my hands forcing things like this. But I've got to know. Will you set up the day for our marriage, or will you not?'

'But I can't!' said the girl.

'Why not?'

'Because of things you can't understand.'

'I'll do my stupid best to comprehend them if you'll try to tell me.'

'But I can't. I can't ... Charles, please wait ... Don't judge me now ... Think of it just for one day ... You're in a passion ... Charles, don't say it!'

'I won't say anything. I'm only waiting for you.'

The voice of the girl came faintly to Kildare, like an agony of his own mind.

'I've known it would have to come to this,' she murmured.

'It doesn't have to come to anything,' declared Herron. 'Ten clear words from you—that's all I want, Nancy.' Then anger got into his voice. 'But you wrong yourself and you wrong me when you trail me like a dog at your heels. Nancy, if it's not our marriage that's making the change in you, will you tell me what else it may be?'

She was silent. As the pause extended, Kildare found that he was holding his breath.

'Very well,' said Herron. 'I'd rather have silence than some lie with nothing but pity behind it. But if you want me to carry on—if you want me to be blind and hopeful—say the word and I'll swallow my pride and be that even.'

There was only the silence again. There was such a tension in Kildare that he felt himself breaking. Every instant of the pause was more incredible to him, for he knew that they loved one another with a rare and deep passion; he could not believe that they were parting. But now he heard Herron saying: 'Losing you is going to be hell, but I'll never come begging for a word and a kind look. You can be sure that you'll never see me again; no matter what happens, you'll never lay eyes on me again.'

Even then she did not utter a word of answer.

When Kildare turned, he saw that Nancy had slipped down into a chair. Herron was taking the house key from his pocket and putting it on the table; then he opened the door and went out. Kildare, hurrying after him, found him lingering an instant on the top step, like someone surveying the weather before venturing out into the city.

Kildare said: 'You're wrong, Herron. She loves you. You're as wrong as the devil. She's not well. She's sick and you're making her desperate.'

It seemed hard for Herron to turn his head so that he could see Kildare. His contempt and disgust he managed to keep unexpressed except by his eyes; then he passed down the steps to his car. Kildare went back to the girl.

Her head had fallen back. She was utterly exhausted. She pulled blindly to get on her gloves.

'You're taking it too hard,' said Kildare. 'That's the way a man is apt to talk to a woman—if he loves her. He'll get over it. He'll come back to you if you say a word.'

She shook her head.

'You don't know him,' she answered. 'He makes up his mind only once about everything.'

'It's not too late, Nancy. You can hurry a message to him. Tell him that you *will* marry him; it's only the setting of the date that's hard on you, just now.'

'Marry him?' she echoed. 'I'll never marry anyone. Will you take me away now? Back to the old house and Nora, Johnny?'

He took her back in the coupé on another silent ride. That word of hers about never marrying had staggered him. He felt that he was being presented not with too little but with too much evidence, only it needed some word, some key for the sorting of it. He wanted time, and apparently there was to be no time, for the action was heaping up before him.

That stunned, unhappy silence continued in her for mile after mile, except that she murmured once or twice: 'I'll never see him again; I'll never lay eyes on him again. Did you hear him say that?'

When they came into the open country, she

had recovered a little. She said: 'Johnny, I know what you think about doctors.'

'They're a silly lot,' he said.

'I know. But it isn't their silliness. When I see one of them, it makes me think of death; it's like having death breathe in my face to have one of them near me. Can you understand that?'

'That's a little thick, but I know that a lot of people feel that way about them,' he agreed. He listened hungrily. There seemed to be many roads toward the solution of the mystery, and this was a promising one. He wanted time, time, time—a month, even a week might do, but the girl, he felt sure, was going now straight to her destiny. This day, perhaps, would end everything.

'But Nora,' said the girl, 'knows someone who is either quite miraculous or else a frightful quack. He hasn't a license to practice. He can't even charge prices for his services. You just give him what you please. Do you think I'd be crazy if I went to him?'

He had struck on the idea of the fear of disease before this as the reason for her state of mind; now her words confirmed him.

'Doesn't it depend?' he asked. 'I mean, don't you have to consider what seems to be wrong with you? What is it, Nancy?'

'Don't ask me. Promise not to ask me about it?'

'Why, of course.'

'It's something that the usual doctors couldn't help. But this man, Nora says, looks in your eyes and knows what's wrong with you. He was away today, but she's located him. After all, it wouldn't be possible for him to do any harm, would it? Not if he simply looked at me and guessed what might be wrong?'

A man practicing without a license, accepting 'gifts' for his services, diagnosing cases by a look into the eyes of the patient exactly fulfilled the definition of a quack, and association with such a fellow or the encouragement or assistance of him in any way by a licensed physician simply removed the doctor from the class of honest practitioners and made a quack out of him in turn. The rules of medical associations and state boards of health were precise on this matter, so precise that Kildare hesitated for an instant as he listened to the girl. He remembered the case of Loder, who had twenty-five years of honorable practice behind him; but when the state board discovered that for three months after receiving his license he had hung out his shingle with a faker, he was drummed out of the ranks. They called Loder a quack because he once had given countenance to a sham doctor; they revoked his license and ruined his life for the sake of those three months which had been used carelessly if not criminally so long before. With that memory in his mind, it was no wonder that Kildare paused for a moment and the girl had to ask again: 'Would I be a fool if I went to such a fellow, Johnny?'

'They're a little ratty, aren't they—fakes like that?'

'I suppose they are.'

'Whereas a licensed physician would at least . . .'

'Physicians—physicians—I know what they do!' she said, a shudder in both voice and body. 'They fill up the house with the thought of death long before death comes. They turn our rooms into coffins. They bury us alive . . . Don't let me talk about them!'

'Forget about them then. And go to this fellow who reads your troubles in your eyes.'

'Shall I, after all?'

'Of course.'

As he made the answer, it seemed to Kildare that all the faces of his old teachers looked in upon him with horror; he heard their voices; he heard the uproar of the great Gillespie sounding above all. A quack is the lowest form of humanity; the very lowest of all. 'Anyone who shall aid, abet, or countenance unsound medical practice, shall not be considered worthy to retain his license.' That was what the book said, and the law stood by to take a corrective hand when need might be.

However, he left his recommendation unchanged as they reached the old country place again. Nora had seen them coming, and she issued from the front door, pulling a coat onto her high shoulders as they drew up before the house. Nancy took the middle place on the seat as her nurse climbed in.

'We'll go right into town,' said Nora. 'Right to the middle of the village, and there you and me can get out, Nancy.'

'Johnny knows where we're going,' said Nancy. 'It's all right.'

'Ah, you told the doctor, did you?' said Nora, persisting in her fancy. She turned her bold eye on Kildare, with as much leer as smile. 'Or maybe he's only a vet.'

Kildare uttered a faint exclamation. Nancy said: 'Nora, Nora, nobody has time for your jokes just now.'

'Ah, but Mr Archbold is no joke, darling,' answered Nora, giving a characteristic switch to the subject. 'There's a man that's a man, and a man's eye in a man's head on his shoulders too. He gives you a look that drops into you like a stone into a pool and scares all the little fish inside you. The doctors said Mrs Winters had stone and wanted to cut her to pieces, bad luck to them, but dear Mr Archbold laid eyes and hands on her and now she's a well woman. And Tad Givens was a failing man for years, with his back bending over and a blink in one of his eyes like too much whisky; but in three treatments didn't Mr Archbold have him fit to climb trees? He was jailed for breaking the peace only the Sunday after. I tell you, there's things that never was in books, and Mr

Archbold has most of them. I've talked to him about you, darling, and he says...'

'I told you not to speak to him about me! I told you not to, Nora. We may as well turn back if you've talked to him about my case beforehand.'

'I spoke only the one word to him,' said Nora, indignant, 'and what harm could there be in that? He knows no more of you than the side of that hill. But in one look he'll see farther than all the rest, you can be sure.'

They came through the little town as a thunderhead rolled up over it and with a downpour of rain covered the hills in a greenish murk of twilight. Nora had the car stopped near the entrance of a building.

'Will you come up with me, Johnny?' asked the girl in a whisper. 'I'm a bit afraid; and I'm almost sure that I'm being a fool.'

He went with her behind Nora up a flight of linoleum-covered stairs and down a dark hallway to the rear of the office building where the single word 'Archbold' appeared on a glass door and under it the legend: 'Personal Advice.' They walked into a small waiting room that was brightened by a window box of late-blooming flowers, and Archbold himself appeared at once from his inner office. The only sign of age about him was the flow of his long white hair. He was a big man, straight as a bolt and with a step like a yearling colt. His bare feet were in sandals; his shirt was open at a hairy throat; and in spite of the sixty years which he must have carried, his eyes were as bright and bold as those of a young lad.

'Ah, Miss Messenger,' he said, and taking her hand he drew himself close to her and lowered the brush of his white eyebrows, inspecting her. 'Your trouble is here—above the eyes—here, I think,' said Archbold, clasping his hand across his own forehead. 'Will you come inside with me?'

That first remark struck Nancy hard. Her lips parted, her eyes aghast, she held back a moment to give one frightened, reproachful glance to Nora. The old nurse said: 'It's all what he sees for himself and nothing that I ever told him. Oh, he's going to blow your troubles away like smoke. Go on in with him, darling.'

So Nancy disappeared through the door, which the hand of the great Archbold closed behind them.

'Now why should you look so scared?' Nora asked, staring at Kildare.

'I hope that he's not a rascal,' said Kildare.

'Trust me for that,' answered Nora. 'I had a terrible pain in my left shoulder and all the tonics wouldn't rub it away, but a touch from dear Mr Archbold turned the trick and I can lie on the left side all night long now and laugh at the doctors in the morning. You wouldn't take me wrong because I've laughed a little in my own way, calling you a doctor, Mr Stevens, would you? Not when my dear girl is like a sister to Johnny; and the kind eye that she lays on you too! But you wouldn't be offended with me, would you, Mr Stevens? The Irish has to come out one way or the other, and God help it!'

CHAPTER FOURTEEN

A slight hubbub of voices in the street called Nora to the window at this moment; she had her nose flat against the glass when the door of the inner office opened again and Nancy came out with the doctor standing huge and bland on the threshold behind her, rubbing his hands together as though to get rid of the excess of good which had just flowed from them. Nancy seemed both bewildered and delighted.

'Not in a moment and not in a touch,' said Archbold, 'but by degrees and little by little we'll do away with it altogether. Remember the order of the three: hope, then faith, then victory. Cleave to that, dear Miss Messenger, and you will see that all will be well.'

In the middle of this speech a trampling approached them down the hall; now the door was pushed open and half a dozen people entered, carrying a lad of twelve or so with a stony face of agony and a rough bandage wrapped around the right leg beneath the knee. Blood dripped from the bandage. Last of the crowd to enter were a frightened man and woman. He was saying: 'Stepped right out from the sidewalk with his head turned back—and the string of fish in his hand—I couldn't dodge him—there wasn't time to get on the brakes . . .'

An elderly man of the village answered in a loud voice: 'I seen you tearing along like a bat out of hell. You took that corner like a wildcat coming off the top of a hot stove, and you know it. There weren't any chance for Billy here to get clear of you. I seen it, and others alongside of me seen it, or ought to have. Mr Speeder, this is gunna cost you a whole pot of money!'

'Don't you go worrying,' said Billy to the accused man. 'I won't make any trouble for you. I was thinking too much about the fish I was carrying.'

Someone was explaining to the great Archbold: 'You're the closest one. You do doctoring or something like it. Take a look to see can you stop that leg bleeding. It's broke plumb bad. It's broke terrible bad!'

Nora took Nancy by the arm. 'We'll get out of here,' she said. 'There's no use taking up space and air where we can't do any good. Mr Archbold will take care of him.'

'Wait, Nora,' said the girl. 'See how brave he is, poor lamb. Why don't they prop up his head a little?'

She was straightway on the floor beside him

with her coat tucked under his head and her handkerchief busy wiping the sweat of pain from his face.

'Fishing? At this time of year?' said Nancy to the boy, smiling.

'You know,' he said. 'Over in the lagoon by the old boathouse.'

'Ah, I remember the old boathouse, but I thought that everybody else had forgotten it,' said Nancy.

'Everybody has,' agreed Billy. 'That's why everything over there is so swell and so still. Nobody ever comes there. Not all year long. And—and—'

Kildare barely heard Nancy murmur: 'Don't try to talk, Billy. I know there's terrible pain, poor old dear!'

He managed to lift his eyes and give her one twisting grin of gratitude; after that, his whole soul was concentrated on that great and terrible ideal of silence, that man-made God or tyrant of those who profess manliness.

The great Archbold, in the meantime, stood for a moment with all eyes fixed upon him. He stood with his legs braced well apart, his arms folded high on his chest and his bushy brows drawn down over his eyes as he stared at the boy.

'We'll see to this,' said the healer and, disappearing into his office for an instant, he came back with a case which he opened, exposing shining rows of steel instruments.

'And now,' said Archbold, 'we'll look into the matter.'

He tossed some cloth to bystanders, saying: 'Just mop the blood up from the floor, will you? If it runs into the corners, you know what blood is—have to tear up the floor to get rid of the signs of it, almost ... Now let me see this young man ...'

So saying, he undid the bandage which had been bound around the leg of Billy in the street below. It was a compound fracture of both bones of the lower leg, the splintered edges thrusting out through the skin. The blood came fast. Three or four of the audience had enough after a single glance and got out hastily.

'An artery!' said the great Archbold. 'And the bones right out through the skin. Too bad, too bad. Except that he's young enough to learn how to use an artificial limb pretty well. But they're never as good as the limbs God gave us.'

Kildare turned his back and looked out the window, trying to forget the damage which ignorance might do to the lad. A moment later, the first sign of pain came from the boy—a low, stifled moan.

Kildare whipped around. Billy, with his eyes closed, blue-white around the mouth, was trying to smile and endure. Archbold seemed to be fumbling aimlessly.

'What will you do to the leg, Doctor

Archbold?' asked Kildare anxiously.

'A tourniquet above the knee, young man,' said the great Archbold, pointing. 'And after the flow of blood has been stopped, the leg must come off at the knee. A pity, isn't it? But better the leg than the life.'

Poor Billy, as he heard this pronouncement, turned his face suddenly toward Nancy, and the girl covered his eyes, holding him close.

'You mean amputation, actually?' said Kildare.

'Mean it? Of course I mean it!' exclaimed Archbold. 'Now if you will give me a little more room, my kind friends . . .'

'You damned butcher!' said Kildare through his teeth.

'Ah? Ah?' cried Archbold. 'What is this?'

Kildare snatched up the medical kit. He said savagely: 'Keep your hands away from him. You rat, don't touch him.'

Then he was on his knees and at work. He had to open the wound first until the blood from the artery was spurting. With a hemostat first dipped in alcohol he clipped the open blood vessel. Hemostat and all he covered with a swift bandage and then arranged the splints. He was halfway through his work when something drew up his eyes involuntarily, and he saw Nancy staring at him in horror. It was only a glance, but it was sufficient to tell him that he had revealed himself and lost his hold on her forever. When his work ended he saw that she was gone from the room.

'We'll get you to my hospital, Billy,' he said, 'and that leg of yours will be fixed so that it'll be as strong as the other one. Will you trust me for that?'

He stood up in time to see the great Archbold disappearing into his inner office; the key sounded in the lock as the miracle man protected the rear of his retreat. But that did not matter now. The ambulance had been telephoned for. In an hour or so Billy would be getting the best care the great hospital could give him.

Somebody was saying: 'This doctor that ain't a doctor—this Archbold that was gunna whip off the leg at the knee—don't he need a little looking into?'

It seemed to be the solemn and grim opinion of the others that this was the truth; but Kildare had no time to listen to them. Nora had caught him by the arm and said: 'Hurry, Mr Stevens. Nancy ain't here. She's gone out to get the air, poor darling, and she mustn't be left alone. Lord God, what a shock it must of been to her to see that you *are* a doctor, after all! If I ever mistrust the Irish in me when it speaks again, call me a fool.'

Kildare went hastily with her down the hallway. The others would see the lad safely in the ambulance, of course, when it arrived.

'When did Nancy leave the room?' he asked.

'I can't say for the life of me,' said the nurse.

'I was that busy watching your fingers do their dance and never tripping themselves up once at all. But oh, Doctor Stevens, or whatever your unlucky name may be, why did you lie to poor Nancy? And who sent you spying on her?'

Kildare did not answer. He got with Nora down to the car they had left in the street, but Nancy was not in it. Her absence was more of a shock to him than to Nora, who said calmly enough: 'Ah, she's gone back to the old house to have a cry—and God forgive you, doctor! But hurry, man, hurry to come to her. She's a nervous girl. She's a terribly nervous girl if there's one in the world.'

They skidded every corner on the way back. When he had jammed on the brakes before the house, he jumped from the car and was already back through the lower floor to the kitchen before the voice of Nora entered the building crying: 'Nancy! Oh, Nancy, darling, where are you?'

She was not on the first floor at least. He raced up to the second and the third story, plunging from room to room, opening even the closet doors. Then he came down to the second story again and found Nora at the top of the stairs leaning against the balustrade with a changed face, haggard and fallen like soft dough.

'Have you a thought where she could have gone?' he asked. 'Can you make a single guess about her?'

'I can make a guess easy enough,' said Nora slowly, drawing her breath in between every word or so. 'There's the railroad bridge that makes a good drop. There's the inlet that's taken more than one unhappy soul before her.'

'She's not done that. She's hidden herself. Try to think if there's a place away from the house where she might have hidden herself; some place she knew when she was a child.'

'What's she now but a child?' demanded the panting voice of Nora. 'The poor innocent—the poor sweet—ah, but you've been the murder and the death of her. God pity the day that she ever saw you, Mr Doctor Stevens or whatever your lying name may be.'

'Try to make sense,' begged Kildare. 'Nora, what's in her mind that drives her frantic?'

'Would *I* be telling you?' demanded Nora. 'God strike me before I'd whisper a word of it. May the black bog take you and keep you. May the mold crawl on the skin of your body! May the heart break and the soul die in you, for you've been the death of my darling!'

Kildare got past her and down the stairs. It would be easy for Nancy to thumb a ride to New York, and it was vastly important that he should get to her father's house before she did. He shot the car down the drive and swung it at a stagger onto the road.

CHAPTER FIFTEEN

The Messenger butler looked at Kildare with an eye of surprise when he opened the door for him.

'Is Mr Messenger here?' asked Kildare.

'He is, and busy,' said the butler. 'But not too busy to see *you*, sir, I'm sure. He's in the library.'

There were unpleasant implications in the tone of this speech. Kildare ran up the stairs and found the library door open. Inside, three men with a bulldog look about all of them sat with Paul Messenger. He was saying: 'You can start your questions. I think I've told the complete story. I'd like to keep it from the newspapers if possible. But if you think the publicity would give us a better chance to find her, I'll call in the reporters.'

He saw Kildare then and, rising from his chair, he moved across the room toward him, saying in his clear, calm voice to the police: 'Excuse me for an instant. I must talk with the doctor who was with her when she disappeared. This is young Doctor Kildare, gentlemen, who seems to have frightened her away.'

He came out to Kildare and closed the door behind him. He was scrupulously polite. He was perfectly cold.

'I have heard from Nora,' said Messenger. 'She tells me that you finally revealed yourself as a doctor and that Nancy, naturally, was frightened away.'

'It was an accident case. I couldn't stand by and see a youngster victimized for life.'

'You found the youngster more important than Nancy?' asked Messenger.

He smiled on Kildare. He was beyond anger.

'You have the police in there, haven't you?' asked Kildare.

'I felt that it was the thing to do. Do you object?'

Kildare said calmly: 'I think that if they come near her, she'll take her life.'

Messenger put a quick hand out and braced himself against the wall, but he rallied at once.

'There is that possibility,' agreed Messenger. 'But from this point forward I prefer the regular to the irregular methods—in spite of the lucky experience of the Chanlers. The police, perhaps the newspapers, will take up where you have left off, doctor.'

'If you use the newspapers, she will know what's coming. She'll kill herself.'

He struck as brutally hard as Messenger and watched the father wince.

After a moment of consideration, Messenger said: 'I think there is only one thing we can reach a mutual agreement upon, and that is to have nothing to do with one another form this point forward. We come to the consideration of your fee. I have my check book here. Kindly name any sum you have in mind.'

'Interns,' said Kildare, 'can't take money.'

'They cannot take money? What *can* you take, Doctor Kildare?'

He answered: 'Nothing!'

'Ah,' said Messenger, 'but you hoped to find advancement in your hospital as a result of your work on this case?'

Kildare considered him through an infinite distance of thought.

'There's no charge to you,' he said.

'You make me uncomfortable,' answered Messenger.

'That's too bad,' said Kildare, still watching him curiously. 'You can repay me in one way.'

'That interests me.'

'Will you tell me the cause of her mother's death?'

'My dear doctor, so far as I am concerned,' said Messenger, 'the case is now in the hands of the police—and perhaps of the newspapers. They may find my daughter for me—since you have lost her.'

'You're hating me,' said Kildare, nodding.

'Not at all,' answered Messenger. '*I* should be punished, not you. The most important work that could be done, I entrusted to a bit of cold blood. I should have searched for a thoroughbred.'

'I understand you,' said Kildare. 'Good-by,

Mr Messenger.'

'Not yet,' insisted Messenger. 'There remains the very important question of remuneration. I cannot take something—whatever it is—for nothing.'

Kildare turned on his heel and left the house.

He went back to the hospital and reported at the office of Carew.

'Messengers with bad news shouldn't be so prompt,' said Carew with his usual hard realism. 'I've heard from our friend Messenger. He seems to think that you've been a bad bargain. Young Doctor Kildare was a valuable article in the Messenger house yesterday, but today there's a bear market on Kildares. As a matter of fact Messenger was in an expansive mood about the whole hospital because of the fine work he thought you were doing. I had him tremendously interested in an extension of our laboratories and some of the most expensive equipment in the world. But of course that's ended now. Why did you scare the girl away, Kildare? You might have thought twice about that, mightn't you?'

He kept tapping at his cigar, though the ashes had not had a chance to form, and looking past Kildare out the window.

When Kildare said nothing, he added: 'Well, there goes a pipe dream out the window. Millions—or nothing. That's the way the world goes ... I suppose you want to be assigned to regular intern duty now that

Gillespie is out of your scheme of things?'

'May I have a day or two off still?' asked Kildare.

'For what?' asked Carew curiously.

'I want to try my luck at finding Miss Messenger.'

Carew tapped his fingers on the desk and frowned.

'That's true,' he said. 'There would be a reward for that.'

Kildare said nothing.

'Irregular,' said Carew, 'but I suppose that I could sanction it. The whole thing has turned out rather badly for you. Tell me one thing, Kildare, will you?'

'If I can, sir.'

'Are you nine-tenths genius or nine-tenths damned fool?... Well, run along.'

Kildare went back to his room, dropped on his bed face down, and slept like an exhausted animal. There was still a gleam of the sunset color in the sky when he wakened, turned, and saw Tom Collins seated on the other bed with a rattling newspaper stretched between his hands.

Collins said, without looking up, 'We hoped you'd get her; but instead of that, you've lost her. Rotten luck, old boy. Gillespie gone, the gal gone; it breaks you down to an ordinary level with the rest of us, doesn't it?'

'You generally have something in that flask of yours, don't you?'

'Generally.'

'Give it to me.'

'Easy on it. This stuff is a lot older than I am.'

Kildare tipped up the flask and drained it. Collins took it, shook its emptiness, and sighed.

'O.K.,' he said. 'I guess you need it. You're tops with me, brother, but you're a yellow dog with the rest of the hospital. By the way, where do you think the Messenger girl can be?'

He held out the newspaper. The disappearance was spilled right across the front page. Detective agencies, boy scouts, and the whole countryside out there in Long Island were looking for her. There was a twenty-thousand-dollar reward.

As Kildare read, Collins kept offering information.

'Don't get in the path of the Cavendish or she'll cut your throat, because it's on account of your leaving, she says, that Gillespie is taking it easy over on Staten Island. And she'd sort of like to keep you away. She thinks you're the death of the old man. I talked to the Lamont girl too. She acts as though she never heard of you.'

'I sold my soul for a mess of pottage, didn't I?' asked Kildare.

'Well, didn't you?'

'I wish there were some more in that flask!'

'Jimmy, don't be so damned smiling and

desperate. There's going to be another day and week and month and year. And you'll be aces high again in the windup.'

'Will you shut up?'

'Sure.'

The telephone rang. His mother's voice took him by surprise on the wire.

'I'm downstairs,' she said. 'Can you see me?'

He wrenched off his clothes, got into whites so that his street dress would not start her asking questions, and hurried down to the reception room. The broad, unbeautiful face of his mother waited for him there. She hugged him, and he held onto her. The good soapy smell which was his earliest memory still clung to her.

'What's wrong?' asked Kildare.

'Nothing, darling. Father had some people to see, so I sneaked over here. We're going to be down for days.'

'What's wrong?' he asked.

'Not a thing I'm telling you. We're going to take some time off.'

'What's wrong?' insisted Kildare.

'Oh, Jimmy. I'm afraid that your father's a sick man.'

'Wait till I get my hat. We'll go over and see him.'

'You can't. He'll hate me if he thinks that I've talked out of school.'

'How does he seem?'

'Jimmy, Jimmy, it's the heart! I swore that I

wouldn't tell you, and now it's out!'

'Everybody has a heart,' said Kildare. 'I'm going over to see him.'

'If you do, he'll know that I've brought you. And he'll never forgive me. Wait till tomorrow. Will you do that?'

'I'll do that.'

'Are you all right, Jimmy?'

'Me? I'm right as rain.'

'There's such a trouble in me that I can't see whether or not you're telling me the truth; but you sound as though you were lying, dear.'

'I'm not lying very much . . . I've got to see father.'

'If he knows you're bothered about him,' said Mrs Kildare, 'he'll turn a lot sicker than he is. I think what steadies him is knowing that while he's going down, you're going up. Ten times a day he starts telling me what Doctor Gillespie is doing for you and what a great man you'll be. If he died tomorrow, he'd die happy. Oh, what a weak fool I am to have come and blabbed to you, darling!'

'Tomorrow. I have to wait till tomorrow, do I?'

'You *will* wait?'

'I'll do what you say. How does he look?'

'It seems to me that there's a shadow in his eye, Jimmy. But maybe, after the report he's had, it's chiefly fear.'

'He's had a report?'

'Don't look at me like that, Jimmy! If God

takes him, it's in God's own time. He's had the life he's wanted, and so long as he knows that you're going on and up toward the top, nothing can make him really unhappy. I want you to think of it that way. And now I must run.'

CHAPTER SIXTEEN

There did not seem to be enough air for breathing, and Kildare's brain made no sense. It kept going around and around like a squirrel in a cage. He could prevent the family from knowing about his disasters for a few hours, but after that the blow would strike them doubly hard. He went up to the roof to see if breathing and thinking might be more possible there, but the fog would not lift from his brain.

After a moment he saw a woman coming toward him, stepping around the chimneys and the ventilators. There was rain-mist in the air so that the glow of New York came straight up from the ground and kept the towers all in a glow. This was the light by which he recognized Mary Lamont.

'I saw you coming up,' she said. 'Do you mind my following?'

'Look,' said Kildare, 'a day or two ago I was riding pretty high. I had the hospital by the heels, and all that. I was going to step into

Gillespie's boots. You know?'

'I know,' she said.

'Now I'm down,' said Kildare. 'I'm socked in the eye. Gillespie hates my heart. Carew has no use for me. Everybody knows that I've tried to sell out for cash, only I wasn't good enough to get by. And somehow that puts in my mind what I wanted to say to you a couple of days ago. I was going to tell you that if you were a few years older and I were making some money, I'd probably ask you to marry me.'

She stepped in close to him. Under her coat he could see the white of her uniform at the throat and there was a dim high light on her cheek and in her eyes.

'You're damned nice,' said Kildare. 'You're going to be gentle and cherishing and all that before you smack me down.'

'Why did you wait till everything went wrong before you talked to me?' asked Mary Lamont.

'I don't know,' he answered. 'I was a fool, I guess. Would you have thought it meant something a couple of days ago?'

She said: 'I'm not very much in your mind. But you're hurt and you want a bit of comfort. Isn't that it?'

'I don't know. You tell me, will you?'

'Are you just going to stand there?' she asked.

He took her in his arms.

'You don't give a damn, but you want to

make me happy,' said Kildare. 'You're rather nice. You're all give and no take.'

He put a finger under her chin and pushed back her head a little, slowly. She made no effort to resist the small pressure.

'Tell me to go to the devil. Don't be a nurse. I'm not so sick,' said Kildare.

'I think you're terribly sick, Jimmy,' she said.

'I'm not,' said Kildare, 'and don't let me maul you around like this. If this keeps on for another minute, you'll be fitted into my mind so that I never can get you out.'

'You'll get me out whenever you want to,' she said.

'I wonder if you'd be damned fool enough to say that you'd marry me?'

'I wonder too,' she said.

'I've got sixty-seven cents a day.'

'I know.'

'I can tell you something that you won't believe.'

'Can you?'

'Yes. I can tell you that I'm almost happy just now.'

'Poor Jimmy!' she said. 'I know.'

'What do you know?'

'That you're in frightful pain.'

He bowed his head until his face was against her hair.

'It's queer, isn't it?' he asked.

'Yes,' she said.

'I mean, it's queer that this should mean such a frightful lot.'

'Yes,' she said.

'Do you know something?'

'What should I know?'

'That you have a beautiful, soft kind of a voice when it speaks close to me like this. It speaks all the way through me. Laugh, now, will you?'

She laughed.

'Do it again,' said Kildare.

She laughed once more.

'You're not so damned beautiful,' said Kildare, 'but you do everything exactly right. Listen to me.'

'Yes?'

'When you came up here, I was sinking for the third time. Now I'm all right. I've had a whiff of oxygen. I know what I've got to do and I'm going to try to do it.'

'Ah, I'm glad,' she said.

'We're breaking the rules all to hell, aren't we?'

'I suppose so.'

'You go down, now. Good night, Mary. Will you go on down now?'

'Yes,' she said.

'And don't you break any rules again.'

'No.'

'I mean, except with me.'

'No,' she said.

She kept looking back at him as she found

her way among the chimneys and the ventilators. Then she disappeared.

* * *

Up in the surgical ward he found Billy and was welcomed by the brightest of smiles. He looked at the chart and spoke to the nurse. The operation had been perfect. Billy, in due time, would walk and run as well as ever.

'You're going to be okay,' said Kildare. 'But you've had some tough luck.'

'I had it coming to me,' answered Billy.

'Coming to you?'

'Sure. I've been a tough guy; now I get the rap. I mean . . . I've always been playing hooky, and pleasing myself, and getting by with a whole lot.'

'School isn't so good, eh?'

'Not so good; but it's going to be better now.'

'That's the stuff,' said Kildare.

'But you know how it seems in the schoolroom when you're studying and there's no sound except somebody scratching his head or pens scraping on paper maybe. It makes you think about going fishing. You know?'

'Of course I know.'

'So I used to go out and get "Jenny"—that's a boat I made—and paddle down the lagoon and hang out a line. You can always get fish in the lagoon. It's fine and lonely down there, and the old wreck of a boathouse, it looks like a murder. You know?'

'I know,' agreed Kildare. 'Places like that are the stuff. They give you something to remember. Are you comfortable?'

'I'm fine . . . and thanks for everything, doc.'

'All right,' said Kildare.

* * *

Collins had a light car. Kildare went up to their room and asked him for it. The telephone called while he was there. A gentleman from the State Board of Health was expecting Doctor Kildare in the waiting room. It was a Dr Oliver Vincent.

'Oliver Vincent—Oliver Vincent,' said Kildare. 'Ever hear of him?'

'Just barely,' said Collins. 'He's the chairman of the State Board of Health. Is *he* down there?'

'He is,' said Kildare, 'and I can guess what he wants to know about.'

'Don't let *him* rattle you,' said Collins. 'The reporters and the police have been on the phone every two minutes for the last hour. I've been in a roommate's hell, brother. Shall I go along and give you a hand?'

'Stay here and pray,' said Kildare, and went down to the office.

The great Dr Oliver Vincent sat in the adjoining room. He was as small as a child, and from a distance his face was that of a child too; but at close range he looked all of his sixty-five years. He had an unpleasant dimple in one cheek, and he seemed always to be smiling, which was an illusion as definitely and heartbreakingly untrue as a mirage in the desert.

Dr Oliver Vincent, whose feet barely reached the floor, turned briskly toward Kildare and made the borrowed desk his own domain.

'Doctor Kildare?' he said. 'You *are* the Doctor Kildare I'm waiting for?'

'Yes,' said Kildare.

'I presume you have not the slightest idea why I am here, young man?'

'I've a very good idea,' said Kildare. 'You want to ask me if I knew that a certain Archbold was not a licensed physician when I took a patient to him, thereby giving aid and assistance and recognition to a quack.'

'Well? Well?' demanded Oliver Vincent.

'There's nothing to say,' said Kildare. 'I've done all of that.'

'Ha?' cried Oliver Vincent. 'And have you the foggiest notion what that may mean to you, sir?'

'I've a perfect idea that it may bar me from practice in this state.'

'You are very calm about this!'

'I've been preparing myself for the firing squad,' said Kildare.

'Young man,' said the chairman of the State Board of Health, 'I presume that you know the authority attached to my position in this state?'

'I know perfectly,' answered Kildare. 'You can and you will scuttle me like an old boat.'

'Your entire attitude,' said Oliver Vincent, 'is not one to conciliate a good opinion. And the case itself is of such importance that I took advantage of my nearness to this hospital in order to run in and see you. You are at perfect liberty, of course, to refrain from answering until you are examined by a more complete authority.'

'I wouldn't dream of it,' said Kildare. 'My goose is already cooked, so why should I give a damn how it is sliced and served?'

'Sir? Sir?' exclaimed Oliver Vincent.

'I mean what I say. I spoke English,' said Kildare. 'You ought to be able to understand me.'

'Can I trust my ears?' shouted Oliver Vincent.

'Suppose I try complete frankness?' suggested Kildare. 'Mr Vincent, I don't give a damn what you do with me and my medical future. You haven't guns big enough to shoot the bullets that are already in me.'

Mr Oliver Vincent considered, rose from his place, and walked silently from the room.

* * *

Kildare took the car he had borrowed from Tom Collins and drove down into the country. The wind that whirred around his windshield went past him like the song of the vanished years. He felt, to use a simile considerably more poetic than any that went through his scientific young mind, like a leaf detached from its twig, still afloat in the air, but about to rejoin the soil of its origin. Life seemed to him a process of decline. Decay was the universal order.

However, he was almost incurably young and far too inconsistent, therefore, to have pleased a romantic poet; and when the moon rose, all glistening bronze like an Homeric shield, he almost forgot that he was a doomed creature. The hope of glory and fame that he had lost, and the great memory of Gillespie, went completely from him. He remembered only Mary Lamont on the roof of the hospital.

He had acquired through excess of pain a peculiar insouciance that denied all the old values and looked for new ones. Still in that humor, he reached the old Messenger place and rang the bell patiently until Nora appeared in an overcoat in place of a dressing gown. She remained within the shadow, only half seen, but even half of Nora was more than enough.

'Ah,' she said, growling like a bulldog. 'It's you!'

'I wanted to know if you've seen her or heard the faintest word from her?' said Kildare.

'If I'd seen her, would I be standing here

blathering?' demanded Nora, and slammed the door in his face.

He drove into the village. They remembered him there. When he stopped his car, twenty people suddenly materialized at the corner.

'There's the *real* doctor,' they said. 'How's that Billy doing, doctor?'

'He's going to have two good legs,' said Kildare. 'Where can I find Archbold?'

'Maybe he's taken wings,' someone said. 'He's not wanted here any longer—the rascal! But nobody's seen him leave his place.'

Kildare went up to the office. He knocked at the Archbold door. He kept at it during ten minutes, at intervals. Presently a key turned and the door opened a mere crack.

'Friends?' said Kildare, when the long nose of Archbold appeared.

The door opened. Mr Archbold waved the way into the room. He had a candle in it, shaded by a large book set up on end so that no ray would reach the window directly and betray him to the street. Mr Archbold had induced in himself a spirit of high good humor.

'Enter, doctor. Enter, enter!' he said. 'Here you will at least find the water of life. May I pour you a drink of it?'

He balanced himself unsteadily, his feet far apart, and proffered a bottle of rye and a glass.

'Good!' said Kildare. 'The water of life is what I need.'

He took the drink, waited for the great

Archbold to pour one for himself, and then toasted him silently.

'I came down to ask you a question,' said Kildare. 'But maybe this is a better way of talking.'

'Undoubtedly,' said Archbold. He rubbed his hands together to get the warmth of the drink thoroughly through his system. 'But what is the question?'

'Ordinarily,' answered Kildare, 'I don't think you do much harm. Maybe the world should have more faith-healers, but not for broken legs.'

'Exactly,' said Archbold. He was so pleased that he gave himself an immediate encore of rye. 'If I had men of understanding around me, doctor, I would be able to take an assured place in this vale of tears, but as a matter of fact I'm a little tired of this damned town. I've been here two years and a half and I know their minds, so-called. I'm ready to move on. I have everything packed and no matter how watchful they wish to be, I'm sure that at about three or four they'll fold their tents and steal away. Then I can be off. They took it very hard, their little discovery of today. But I don't hate you because you revealed me, doctor. No malice in me whatever.'

'Thank you,' said Kildare. 'After all, I knew that you couldn't do the girl any harm.'

'Of course not,' said Archbold, laughing. 'No harm and no good. Who can do any good for a malignant tumor of the brain?'

Kildare took a deep breath. He had at last the information he wanted.

'I wonder what convinced her that she had that?' he asked.

'Ah, the nurse told me enough about that,' explained Archbold. 'Imagine her own mother dying of the same disease. And the house filled with doctors and nurses for years until the girl came to hate the whole medical profession. You see?'

'I begin to,' said Kildare.

'And once, before the end, the child heard her mother's voice—babbling—making no sense—you understand? The mind of the poor woman had given way, I suppose. So the horror was born in Nancy. Very affecting, I'm sure. When her headaches began she inquired and learned the nature of her mother's illness. Of course the headaches seemed proof that she had the same thing. And the other day when she told that fat-brained Irish nurse about her symptoms, of course Nora jumped to the conclusion that the end was upon her. The fool told the girl a few of the details about the mother's death. Clear and simple, the whole thing, isn't it?'

'Perfectly.' said Kildare.

He got down to the street and the car quickly.

CHAPTER SEVENTEEN

But when he was in the car, for all his haste he realized that he had no destination. Probably he already was too late and somewhere within the round of the hills Nancy lay dead. He took the first road, then another right, another left, and saw the lights of a village rising before him like a patch of ragged stars. The town he drove into was the same that he had left. He had driven in a blind circle.

He saw before him now the corner at which Billy had been injured, and at the sight of it his mind went forward to the picture of the lad stretched on the floor of Archbold's office with Nancy sitting beside him. There had been such beauty in her then that he always would remember her, he knew, as she had been in that moment. He could remember every word that had passed between her and Billy about the old boathouse to which no one came throughout the year, a forgotten place lost in the woods beside a lagoon. Remembering that, a new light of hope flashed on in his brain. He pulled up the car at the curb and asked a bystander the way to the old boathouse.

'Old boathouse? There's the boathouse down at the pier. That's the only one I know about,' said the man on the corner.

'Down by a lagoon, lost in the woods—the

old boathouse. Doesn't anyone remember it?' asked Kildare, anxiously scanning the faces as a group gathered on the pavement.

A farmer with a red face that glistened with whisky and his weekly shave now answered: 'Ain't that the place over there beyond the end of the Brighton Road? Sure it is. You'll miss it if you don't look sharp. Right down there—where the Road makes a right turn and an old lane runs on . . .'

Kildare found the Brighton Road and then the old lane at the turn.

Before he knew it, he was driving through a thick forest that shut out the light of the moon and left him in a dense winter blackness. The air turned cold and damp. Through the woods he came out upon a curving lake, silver under the moon, that blocked all forward progress unless he took, to the side, a narrow way that wound through the slums of tree roots and obscurity. Kildare put on the brakes and stared vaguely before him at a little boat, leaning crazily to one side, which swung at the end of an improvised pier. It was veering with the wind. Something like a reflection from the moon-brightened water was visible on her side, aft. Now it appeared to suit a craft of ten times her tonnage. The word it spelled was 'JENNY.'

He remembered Billy then, though in fact Billy had said that his homemade boat was moored in front of the boathouse. That was why he looked about with more care and saw it at last. The roof was so fallen in ragged patches that it gave an upper outline like a portion of the woods; but now that he looked more closely, he could see the dark blink of the windows. When he tried to start, a rear wheel bit into the sand, hollowed a place for itself, and refused to climb out of the hole it had excavated.

Kildare got out of the car and set about looking for a fragment of wood with which he could clear the earth away and give the wheel a start. He was well at work when a chill came upon him from behind. He looked with fixed eyes over the bright face of the water, then jerked his head around and saw the figure moving straight toward him from the ruin of the boathouse. It came on with a hesitant step, both hands stretched forward, the head held high and the face tilted upward so that the moon shone full on the face of Nancy Messenger. As he watched, she came behind a ragged stump of a pine tree. She walked straight on like a creature without sight. Horror took him by the throat. It seemed as though the wretched little tree possessed life, malevolence, and will of its own to move and to strike. The girl walked full into it and the blow struck her to her knees.

He could not stir, but Nancy, gathering herself patiently, rose again. With her outstretched hands she found a way around the tree and came on toward the water. He could tell then why her eyes, helplessly wide, were fixed upon the moon. There was no sight in them. He had to try once or twice before her name would come past his lips.

* * *

The voice of Carew as it had shrilled over the telephone kept sounding and resounding in the ears of Messenger all the way to the hospital. When he reached the place, Carew in person met him at once.

Carew said: 'A most extraordinary piece of work, but then we're used to extraordinary work from Kildare. You know the quality of the genius, Mr Messenger? He seems more commonplace than the most ordinary person—until he turns the trick again. He's just another batter at the plate until he knocks the home run.'

'You've seen Nancy?' said Messenger. 'Is it actually true that her sight is gone?'

'The present symptoms,' said Carew, 'seem to indicate blindness. But let's not be too absolute. Doctor Kildare is right in here. Right through this door, Mr Messenger.'

'I don't think I can face him,' said Messenger. 'I've been too frank with him—too brutally frank.'

'Ah, I understand perfectly,' said Carew. 'You think that, being offended, he won't forget. The quality of the genius, on the other hand, is that he is aware, not of you or me, but only of the case in hand. You'll see at once!'

Messenger, entering the small office behind Carew saw a surprisingly pretty nurse who came to attention with level, bright eyes.

'Where's Kildare?' asked Carew.

'He's in the next office, sir,' said Mary Lamont.

'Call him here at once,' directed Carew.

'Yes, sir,' said the nurse with a troubled face, and disappeared into the next room.

Messenger heard the voice of the girl speaking, and then that of Kildare answering: 'Tell them to go hang ... Look, Mary! I think I've got it! See those mice in there? They were getting too much interval between injections. I've cut it down to a quarter, and now look at 'em! They've had enough of the stuff to kill them ten times over, but not a one of them is drooping even.'

'You're right,' said the girl. 'Would Doctor Gillespie—'

She stopped herself.

'Oh,' said Kildare, 'he'd be glad even if *I* turned the trick. There's no malice in him, Mary, where medicine is concerned.'

'I know there isn't,' she said, 'but now there's Doctor Carew and Mr Messenger waiting for you in the outer office ...'

Kildare came out suddenly. He overlooked Carew and went up to Messenger.

'The police—the newspapers—the boy

scouts—the whole of them failed,' said Messenger. 'But *you* didn't fail, Kildare. If you'll permit me to unsay certain things that…'

'We have one interest in common, and that's Nancy,' broke in Kildare. 'Why humiliate yourself making excuses? I don't want them. If we can help her, we'll be helping one another. And we're ready to do that, aren't we?'

'I was frightfully wrong,' said Messenger.

'You were dealing with a very sick girl,' said Kildare. 'And because you're not a doctor, you had a right to be wrong … Excuse me a moment…'

He hurried back into the inner office.

'He seems deeply depressed. Is it because of the condition of Nancy?' asked Messenger of Mary Lamont.

'No, it's not that,' she said, and looked at Carew.

Carew explained, shrugging his shoulders: 'I suppose being in the office depresses him. It was here that he was being taught by Gillespie until he gave up all that.'

'It seems to me,' said Messenger forcefully, 'that that young man needs the teaching of no one. He seems to be able to go on by himself. Am I wrong?'

'Yes, sir,' said Mary Lamont.

'You mean that this Gillespie is a sort of god from the machine—a kind of prophet for Kildare?'

‘Yes, sir,’ said Mary Lamont.

‘Will he take me up to see Nancy now?’

‘Yes, sir.’

‘Will you kindly tell me what’s keeping him in there just now?’

‘Some white mice, sir,’ said Mary Lamont.

* * *

Kildare leaned over the X-ray plates and pointed out the details to Messenger. He had drawn a crude sketch of the course of the optic nerves to make the ideas clearer.

‘They come from back in the brain in two branches,’ said Kildare, ‘and they converge toward this shadow, which is the pituitary gland. The pituitary is an out-pocketing of the brain fitted into a sort of cup, the pituitary fossa. If you look very closely here, you’ll see two small projecting shadows.’

‘I see them,’ nodded Messenger.

‘They’re at the top of the pituitary gland, you see, and they’re called the clinoid processes. They’re important to us just now. The point is that Nancy *suddenly* lost her sight. It wasn’t a gradual dimming. One day she had full vision; the next day she was totally blind. That’s extremely unusual unless there has been an accident directly to the eyes themselves. But one can imagine that a sudden enlarging of a tumor of the pituitary gland might interrupt the course of the two optic nerves at this point where they converge. That would explain the quick loss of vision. In case of such a tumor, one should see the two little growths of bone—the clinoid processes—pushed up. Now turn back to the lateral plate of the skull again. You see in fact that the clinoid processes are somewhat elevated...'

'It means there *is* a tumor then?' demanded Messenger in a shaken voice.

'There is a great deal against the idea of a tumor. The pituitary may be simply slightly enlarged, but not a malignant growth. If there were a tumor which had interrupted the optic nerve, an exterior examination of the eye should show that the heads of the nerves are in a pathological condition, dead or dying. However, the nerve heads seem perfectly normal. As for tumors in other parts of the brain, there would have to be two: one in each lobe, each suddenly increased in magnitude so that on the same day each branch of the optic nerve was damaged. This would be a miraculous improbability.'

'Then what *is* the explanation?'

'I don't know,' said Kildare. 'There are no other signs of tumors except the headaches; there are no tokens of any paralysis in the muscles around the head and neck which are supplied by the cranial nerve. Mind you, we are not quite sure about the exact condition of the pituitary gland at this moment. We are taking more pictures.'

'There's only one definite fact, so far as I can understand the thing,' said Messenger. 'That fact is that she has lost her eyesight completely.'

'She has,' agreed Kildare.

'Is there the least hope?'

'I don't know. To exterior examination the eyes are normal. That's the great point in our favor. *I* have hope; the others are noncommittal.'

Messenger lighted a cigarette with a shuddering hand. He was trembling slightly from head to foot.

'All we can do is wait?' he asked.

'And work,' added Kildare. 'We have to find out the facts as absolutely as possible and then consider what is to be done next.'

'May I see her now?'

'I'll find out,' said Kildare, and went into the room. Mary Lamont was there arranging flowers in a great vase. The empty eyes of Nancy were turned to the other girl as she said: 'Why do you bother? I can't see them, you know.'

'They make the air sweet,' answered Mary, 'and then you can hear the wind rustling in them.'

'Has someone just come into the room?' asked Nancy.

'Only Doctor Kildare.'

'Ah, are you here again?' murmured Nancy. 'Do I have to learn a new name for you,

Johnny?'

'No . . . I have to speak to you, Miss Lamont.'

'Are you going to leave me, Johnny?'

'I'll be back in a moment.'

In the hall, Mary Lamont said: 'Now I know why you left Doctor Gillespie. I was fool enough to think that it was money and all that; but now I know it was Nancy Messenger. And she's lovely. She's *lovely*, Jimmy!'

'What are you talking about?' demanded Kildare. 'Are *you* going to be a damned fool?'

She stared at him. 'It isn't . . .' she murmured.

'It isn't what?' he snapped.

'I don't know,' she said faintly.

'Try to make sense, will you, Mary?'

'Yes, I'll try.'

'Tell me what she was doing when you came up.'

'She was staring at the ceiling and thinking. If I'd been a lip reader I could have made out her thoughts.'

'Black, were they?'

'Jimmy, she's going to die!'

'Nonsense!'

'She doesn't want to live.'

'That can be fixed.'

'How, Jimmy?'

'By cutting out her will to die and transplanting a will to live,' he said harshly. 'Just a little operation. That's all. What's her appetite?'

'She can't eat. She won't eat, Jimmy . . . Poor girl! She's so sweet, Jimmy!'

'Stop crying about her, will you?'

'Yes, Jimmy.'

'I want a bright attitude in that room. I want cheer and hope and all that sort of rot. You understand?'

'Yes, doctor.'

'You can help because you're her kind.'

'Yes, doctor?'

'Thoroughbred, I mean,' said Kildare, and went back into Nancy's room.

'If you don't eat,' said Kildare, 'I'm going to forcefeed you like a Strasbourg goose. You hear?'

'I'll never see him again,' said Nancy. 'Never, never, never! . . . Will you come over to me a little closer, Johnny?'

'I'm not going to let you cry all over me,' said Kildare. 'I won't have any of this damned nonsense.'

'Ah, I wish the old Johnny were back with me!' sighed Nancy. 'He understood—everything.'

'I have some news for you,' said Kildare, standing over the bed and staring down at her. She felt this nearness and touched him with a groping hand and smiled faintly.

He went on: 'We've completed the X-ray pictures and the tests practically. There's only one thing we're sure about. There is no brain tumor, malignant or otherwise.'

She caught her hands back to her face and gasped, looking into the darkness of her world with bewilderment.

'But that's not true,' she said at last. 'You'd say anything to make me happy. You can't fool me with your grimness, Johnny. I've looked so far into you that I've seen your heart.'

'Damn my heart,' said Kildare.

He took a quick breath, set his teeth, and then said: 'I give you my professional word of honor—whatever is wrong with you, it's not what caused your mother's death. Think that over and try to stop acting like a halfwit.'

He turned his back on her and got hastily into the adjoining room where Messenger waited. Carew was there, with the eye-specialist, Landon, and the great brain man, McKeever.

'They tell me it's a very dark mystery, doctor,' said Messenger anxiously. 'May I go in to see her only for a moment?'

'No,' answered Kildare. 'She needs a bit of time to digest some good news.'

He looked straight across the room at McKeever.

'I've just told her,' he said, 'that there is no brain tumor.'

'But, my dear fellow,' protested McKeever gently, 'can you go as far as that? Can you be sure of that at the present moment? Admitting the general indications are favorable...'

'I've given her my professional word of

honor that there is no brain tumor,' said Kildare.

'But is that ethical?' demanded Landon with suddenly rising anger.

Messenger, deeply troubled, looked from one of them to the other.

'I'm not thinking of ethics. I'm thinking of Nancy Messenger,' said Kildare.

'Young man—I wonder if you always remember how very young you are?' asked Carew darkly.

'I know your instinct and your way, Doctor Kildare,' said the gentle voice of old McKeever, as he smiled on the boy. 'You fight with the point and with the edge and you give no quarter. You'll take big chances if you think the patient may profit by it. But . . . considering this entire case . . .'

He allowed his voice to die out.

Kildare gestured to Messenger.

'You've put this case in my hands,' he said. 'Technically, that's impossible. An intern can't have absolute control of *anything* in a hospital. I think I see my way a step or two ahead through the fog of this case, but only dimly. I've not much more than instinct to go on just now—but I've made a definite statement to your daughter. If you want that statement retracted, you can take the authority away from me with a single word.'

He turned his back on all of them and went to stare out the window.

'With all due respect to young Doctor Kildare,' said Carew, 'and considering how *very* young he is, I cannot help pointing out to you that in this room with you are two of the finest specialists that can be…'

'No, Carew. No, Walter,' said old McKeever. 'The boy has a great heart and a fine mind. Why not let him have his chance? The rest of us have little or no light to throw on the problem.'

'It's a hard decision for me to make,' said Messenger. 'I realize that Kildare is not the oldest man in the world, but it's my habit in business to put my trust in the people who win. When I had the whole world searching for Nancy, he reached into the dark and brought her back to me… Kildare, the case is entirely in your hands.'

'Thank you,' said Kildare, suddenly facing them again.

Old McKeever went and laid a hand on his shoulder.

'Use me in any way you can, my dear boy,' he said. 'I'm at your service.'

* * *

But a greater help than even McKeever could give was what Kildare needed. He went to find Gillespie.

Staten Island, which seems a hundred years behind the times, is not famous for its beaches.

Nevertheless there is a stretch of seaside that looks out over blue water toward the jumbled heights of Manhattan. Dr Gillespie sat in his wheel chair on the edge of the sand with the rush and foaming of the waves just before him. Conover held an umbrella over him.

'The legend of the seventh wave being the largest,' said Gillespie, looking up from a notebook in which he had been making marks, 'is definitely wrong.'

'Yes, sir,' said the big Negro.

'It must be dismissed from all minds as pure tradition and bunk,' insisted Gillespie.

'Yes, sir,' said Conover.

'Tradition and legend,' said Gillespie, 'is the embalmed idiocy accumulated by the ages.'

'Yes, sir.'

'It is the enemy of science.'

'Yes, sir.'

'There is a man,' said Gillespie, 'heading directly toward us. It is probably a reporter.'

He relaxed in his chair.

'Make signs to him,' said Gillespie, 'that I'm asleep.'

He closed his eyes.

'It's no good, sir,' said Conover.

'What the devil do you mean it's no good?' demanded Gillespie angrily.

'He'll see right through your closed eyes,' said Conover. 'There ain't any fooling him. Not about you, sir. It's Doctor Kildare.'

The footfall came through the whispering

sands of the beach.

'Doctor Gillespie,' said the voice of Kildare, 'may I speak with you for a moment?'

'You may not,' said Gillespie.

'How are you, Conover?' said Kildare.

'I'm fair to middling, sir,' said Conover.

'Can I do anything to make him talk to me?' asked Kildare.

'The doctor ain't taken a very full breakfast, sir,' said Conover. 'Maybe if you was to wait till after lunch . . .'

'Conover, shut your mouth!' commanded Gillespie.

'Yes, sir,' agreed Conover. 'If you was to wait up at the hotel till lunch time, Doctor Kildare . . .'

'The Messenger girl is back in the hospital, sir,' said Kildare. 'She's convinced that she has the same disease that killed her mother—a malignant tumor of the brain. The evidence is against that, but the fact is that *something* has made her blind.'

'Conover!' roared Gillespie.

'Yes, sir,' replied the Negro.

'Tell this damned interloper that I prefer to be alone.'

'The doctor says that he'd like to take a nap, sir; I'm sorry to say, sir,' interpreted Conover.

'If you possibly could spare the time to look at her,' said Kildare, 'I will have her brought to you here, sir.'

'Conover!' roared Gillespie.

'Yes, sir?' asked Conover.

'Wheel me down the dammed beach! Get me away from this.'

He turned the wheel chair as he spoke.

'Why don't you go on, Conover, you jackass?' cried Gillespie.

'Doctor Kildare has done got his hand on the back of the chair, sir.'

'A damned impertinent outrage!' cried Gillespie. 'Strike his hand away and march on.'

'I'm terribly sorry, sir,' said Conover. 'Maybe I ain't man enough to do that.'

'Did you wink at this fellow when you said that, Conover?' shouted Gillespie.

'Oh, no, sir!'

'You lie!' thundered Gillespie. 'You're a liar and the father of liars.'

'The best advice in the hospital, sir,' said Kildare, 'is that the optic nerve seems entirely normal and the reactions show no signs of any deterioration of the corneal nerve. If you'll permit me to bring her to you ...'

'Conover!'

'I beg your pardon, Doctor Kildare,' said Conover.

'All right,' said Kildare.

The wheel chair began to move slowly over the sand, impelled by Conover.

'You don't need me any longer, young Doctor Kildare,' cried Gillespie. 'You don't need the advice of any man. You found your way into the long green that means so much to you. You can bed yourself down in it now! And God give you comfort in it. But don't come with your whining questions to me again as long as you live!'

There was no answer.

'Are we far from him, Conover?' the diagnostician asked.

'Yes, sir.'

'Then get me back to the hotel and find out the next ferry for New York. Hurry, Conover! You black scoundrel, you're fired. I won't have you any longer. I'm going to get me a young man with some life in his legs and brains in his hands. You hear me?'

'Yes, sir,' said Conover.

CHAPTER EIGHTEEN

Young Doctor Kildare stood in line and took his chances in front of that office door where he had so often assisted or presided. Conover said at last: 'You're next, sir.'

And Kildare entered and found himself looking down into the formidably bent brows and eyes of Gillespie.

'What's wrong with *you*?' demanded Gillespie.

'Nothing, sir.'

'Then get out! What do you think this is? A social hour, or what?'

Kildare backed slowly toward the door.

'I hoped that you'd able to see my father, sir. His doctors think that there has been a coronary occlusion . . .'

'And what do *you* think?' demanded Gillespie.

'I feel that they're wrong, sir.'

'Reasons, please. Feelings haven't a damned thing to do with medicine.'

'I don't presume to know. But if I were a practicing doctor I would send the case to you, sir.'

Gillespie said: 'Send him elsewhere. His name is against him here. Kildare, there once was a man who had twelve disciples. It was a tragedy when one of the twelve betrayed him. I have had *one* disciple. And that one betrayed me. Do you understand?'

'I understand,' said Kildare, and got out of the great man's sight.

He stood in the waiting room for a moment while his brain cleared. The voice of Mary Lamont said: 'I don't think that he meant it all, doctor.'

'He meant every word of it,' said Kildare.

'I told him what you have been doing in the experiment, and he was frightfully interested,' she said.

'Was he?' asked Kildare wearily. 'Nevertheless, he despises me.'

'Will you let me try to explain?'

'No,' said Kildare. 'Nobody can explain him

to me. If I don't know *him*, I know nothing. Mary, did he go to see Nancy Messenger?'

'Yes,' she said. 'This morning.'

'Did he say anything?'

'Not a word.'

* * *

The day grew to the afternoon, and the interns of the big hospital sat in well-ordered rows before Gillespie, once more back on the job. Pens or pencils staggered rapidly across notebooks as the young doctors tried to keep pace with the outpourings of the great man. In the rearward row sat Kildare.

'... hysteria that can take the place of almost any disease,' he was saying. 'There is a simulation that almost passes understanding. A feature is the glove anesthesia, which will begin in the hand and spread over it, a total senselessness to all impressions ... we have cases of people struck mute, and people who suddenly grow deaf ... The mind and the nervous system are the tyrants over the body.'

The elect among the interns generally sat up in front, close to the lecturer, making their notes. Toward the rear were those who came more from a sense of duty than in real hope to learn. From among these Kildare suddenly sprang to his feet, snatched the door open, and was gone from the room.

'Who the devil left this room? Who left that

door open?' shouted Gillespie.

'It was Doctor Kildare, sir,' said an intern, hastily rising to close the door at the rear of the room.

'Ha?' said Gillespie. 'He's been doing a little deducing, has he? Well, brains *will* show themselves in spite of the devil.'

Kildare, opening the door of Nancy's room a trifle, carefully beckoned Mary Lamont out to him into the hall. She had been sitting close to the bed of her patient, talking with animation.

'How is she?' asked Kildare.

'Much better. She's eaten something. Her whole temper is better.'

'If you were the doctor, how would you describe her present condition, frankly?'

'I'd say that it's a minor improvement in a hopeless case.'

'Would you?'

'Yes, doctor.'

'You were interesting her just now.'

'Yes, doctor.'

'What were you talking about?'

The answer came up in her eyes and stopped there without words. She flushed.

'Is it none of my business?' demanded Kildare.

'Yes, doctor.'

'Get Mr Charles Herron on the telephone and ask him if he can come to the hospital at once to consult with me about Miss

Messenger. *If* he can come, ask Landon and McKeever, if they can give me a few moments at a conference. I'll want Mr Messenger also.'

'He's always in the next room waiting for a call, doctor.'

'Is he? By the way, the great Carew probably would want to be at that conference. You might tell him.'

'Yes, doctor.'

'That's all,' said Kildare, and went on into Nancy's room.

'Johnny?' she asked.

'You're a mind reader,' said Kildare. 'You can see in the dark, so you don't need eyes; but you're going to have them anyway.'

She sat up in the bed with an exclamation.

'What have you found?' she asked.

'I've found,' said Kildare, 'that when you sit up like that and smile you're a lovely girl to look at, Nancy.'

'Ah, I like that!' she said. 'If there were only more nonsense like that in you, Johnny! . . .'

'Well, what?'

'You could make more people happy. Particularly . . .'

'Particularly who?'

'What is it you found out?'

'That I'm going to have to knock you out for three days.'

'Ah?' she said indifferently, sinking back in the bed once more. 'What's going to happen to me while I'm asleep?'

'Some rather painful applications to the eyes … When you wake up, there'll still be a bandage across those eyes … Nancy, you didn't believe me when I told you that there was no brain tumor?'

'No, Johnny.'

'Will you believe me if, when I take the bandage off your eyes, you see?'

'Johnny, I know that you're not simply encouraging me. You mean what you say this time?'

He had to close his eyes to shut out the sight of her. Still with his eyes closed, he said: 'I mean it! You're going to see! Full vision in both eyes.'

She put her hands up over her face. 'I'm going to try to believe,' she said.

'I don't care whether you believe or not,' said Kildare. 'Set yourself against it, and you'll have all the more pleasure when those bandages are taken off. Surprise is one of the first elements in real pleasure, isn't it? … I'm going to give you an injection that will knock you galley-west. Shall I put the bandage over your eyes before or after you go to sleep?'

'After,' she said. 'I don't want you to sit there looking at me when I'm wrapped up like an Egyptian mummy. I'm terribly vain, Johnny, and I'm sentimental about you besides.'

He prepared her arm and gave the barbital injection.

'You're going to sleep fast,' he said. 'If you have any talking to do, do it now.'

'I want Nora here when I wake up.'

'She has a lot of wrong ideas.'

'I know. But I love her, and she loves me.'

'I'll have her here when you wake up.'

'Thank you . . . Johnny, when you talked to me about the hell that *you* were going through, it was all made up, wasn't it? There wasn't a word of truth in it?'

'There was more than a word of truth in it. I was in a different sort of hell. That was all.'

'I knew that there was something. Are you happy now, Johnny? Is all the sorrow gone from you?'

'You're the patient, not I.'

'I wish you could tell me about it. You can't be sure that I wouldn't be able to help.'

'I'll tell you about it when you're on your feet, able to look me in the eye, and happy.'

'Happy? Do you think that I can ever be *happy* again?'

'Leave that to me too,' said Kildare.

'I almost think I could,' said the girl. She yawned. 'Johnny,' she murmured, 'you're the only friend in the world. Nobody else—nobody knows—how—to be—a friend . . .'

She was asleep. Kildare went into the next room, where Messenger stood up at once and passed him a check.

He said to Messenger: 'What's this?'

'A small retainer, doctor,' said Messenger.

'Interns can't accept fees,' explained Kildare.

'There was a reward offered for the finding of Nancy,' argued Messenger.

'Finding her was merely a part of my medical duty in the case,' said Kildare.

'I've learned a little about what has happened to you in this hospital,' said Messenger, 'and what you gave up in order to take the case of Nancy. If you didn't expect to get some financial return, will you tell me what induced you to make the change?'

'It's one of those things that don't stand talking.'

'If you can't take this check, will you throw the thing away? . . . Give it to the next beggar on the street—but don't ask me to take it back.'

Kildare crumpled the check blindly in the palm of his hand. He forgot it.

'How long will it take you to bring Nora here?' he asked.

'She's in town. I can have her here in half an hour.'

'Please send for her then. Tell her that Nancy is going to have her sight restored.'

Messenger left in haste for Nora; when Mary Lamont hurried into the room a moment later, she found Kildare sitting at the center table bowed over a book in which there was a complicated chart of the eye in colors. He was lost in the study of it.

She said breathlessly: 'Doctor Gillespie has

sent for your father.'

'Don't bother me,' said Kildare.

'Your father is with him now,' said Mary Lamont.

'With who?' said Kildare.

'With Doctor Gillespie.'

'I'm busy,' said Kildare. 'Who is with Doctor Gillespie?'

'Dr Stephen Kildare,' said Mary Lamont.

'Doctors ought to stay away from Gillespie,' said Kildare. 'He has enough to do handling the laymen.'

'Did you understand the name I gave you, doctor?'

'Damn the names. I don't care about the tags. Get Herron for me. Mary, wait a minute. Here's a check or something from Messenger. The fool won't understand that interns can't take money. Give it where the giving will do the most good. Or—wait a minute—keep it yourself.'

He bowed his head over the book again.

'The other doctors will be in this room within an hour, doctor,' she said, shaking her head helplessly as she stared at him. 'And Mr Charles Herron...'

'What about him? I want Herron!' said Kildare.

'He's waiting to see you now,' said the girl.

'Bring him here!' snapped Kildare.

He was walking up and down the room when Herron came in. The big man had about the face a bruised and battered look that made him seem older and sterner. He came to Kildare, took his hand, and made an instant apology.

'The last time I spoke with you, I misunderstood your position, Doctor Kildare,' he said, 'and my treatment of you . . .'

'That's finished and done with,' said Kildare. 'Let's not waste time on it. I'm only glad you didn't break me in two and throw the pieces away. I could see that was what you wanted to do . . . Herron, I haven't time to be polite and indirect. There was a time when you loved Nancy Messenger. She put you through a bad time and your temper wore out. When you told her she never was to see you again, you meant it.'

'I was hurt, and I acted like a child. That was all.'

'Herron, do you mean to say that you weren't speaking your real mind? Does she still mean something to you?'

'More than I dreamed she did before.'

'I'm going to need your help. Can I use you?'

'Use me? God knows you can!'

'Then stand by,' said Kildare. 'I'll tell you your lines when the time comes.'

Mary Lamont took the twenty-thousand-dollar check down to Gillespie. When she went into the outer office she heard him saying: 'They all agreed?'

'Yes, doctor,' the gentle voice of old Dr Stephen Kildare was answering.

'All agreed that it was heart?'

'Yes, doctor.'

'Why, damn my soul, Kildare,' said Gillespie, 'the fact of the matter is that you *have* a mortal illness, but it isn't your heart at all. There hasn't been a coronary occlusion. There's only been an attack of indigestion ... Don't spend as much time over your wife's cooking—and take some sodium bicarbonate now and then.'

'Really?' said the old country doctor. 'But the mortal illness?'

'Incurable,' said Gillespie. 'You're an old man. And God and all his angels can't keep you from dying of old age ... That's all that's wrong with you, you fool!'

Mary Lamont waited for the exit of the old doctor before she went to Gillespie.

The tyrant said: 'I thought that you were back on general duty. What are you doing here, Lamont?'

'I'm here to shame you,' said the nurse.

'I've stood a lot in my life,' said Gillespie, 'but I've never had to stand the hysterical jitters of a probation nurse. Not before this moment.'

'I have this for you,' said Mary Lamont, and put on the desk before him a sadly crumpled piece of paper.

'What is it?' asked Gillespie, peering.

'This says twenty thousand dollars and Paul Messenger's signature makes it mean what it says.'

'It's made out to Kildare,' said Gillespie. 'I see what you mean, Mary. You're giving me an object lesson in how to be a doctor and how to take in the spoils at the same time. Is that it?'

'Look!' said the girl. 'He's endorsed it and handed it to me . . . to give away . . . to any charity . . . or keep for myself. He doesn't care.'

'Don't try to make a fool of me,' snarled Gillespie. 'This fellow Kildare would give his soul for hard cash. He wants nothing out of life except the long green . . . He wouldn't give this away . . . But he has,' said Gillespie.

He crumpled the check between both his hands suddenly and stared at the girl.

'What are you saying to me?' cried Gillespie. 'Are you trying to make an absolute doddering idiot of me? Are you trying to tell me that he had some secondary purpose? What was it, Lamont? What was it?'

'I don't know,' said the nurse. 'But you were a very sick man a few days ago.'

'Is that it?' said Gillespie softly. 'I remember shouting him down when he told me that I had to rest. So he took the tools for work out of my hands. He simply removed himself without explanation and left us here damning him.'

'Yes, doctor,' she answered in a trembling voice.

'Stop that sniveling!' snarled Gillespie.

'Yes, doctor,' she said.

CHAPTER NINETEEN

For the hospital, it was a large room. The flowers were everywhere, but even flowers, even fields of them, cannot take the entire curse from a hospital room.

After all, it was not the impersonal environment on which Kildare intended to depend. He stood by the bed and looked down at the girl for a moment. She had one bare arm thrown up over her head. Thick bandages swathed the upper part of her face. On the other side of the bed stood Nora, looking from Nancy to Kildare like a frightened child at a schoolteacher. He said to her: 'Nora, you're rather a blatherskite.'

'Yes, sir. Yes, doctor,' said Nora.

'But if so much as once you mention her mother or her mother's death to Nancy while you're with her, I'll have you boiled in oil.'

'Yes, sir,' said Nora.

Kildare turned on his heel and went into the adjoining room. Landon and McKeever were there with Carew and big Charles Herron. Paul Messenger walked nervously up and down, halting suddenly when he saw the intern.

Kildare said abruptly: 'I've put Miss Messenger to sleep and bandaged her eyes. I've told her that when she wakes up she will have had three days of treatments to her eyes—and that when the bandages are removed, she will have perfect vision.'

Messenger and Herron exclaimed softly. The doctors said nothing at all. They merely looked at one another.

Kildare said: 'The X-ray plates and the physical examination practically remove all possibility that there can be a tumor or any lesion affecting the optic nerve. The eyes seem normal, and following a suggestion indirectly made by Doctor Gillespie, it seems to me that Miss Messenger's blindness may be attributed to hysteria. In a moment of great emotional stress she was told by Mr Herron that she never would see him again; she never would lay eyes on him again. The thought persisted in her mind. She kept repeating the word. The idea entered her deeply. Afterward, she received an unpleasant shock when she discovered that I was a doctor and therefore, she felt, established as a spy upon her life. She ran away and hid herself, prepared to take her own life. Then the hysteria overtook her suddenly. She went blind. I have given her enough barbital to put her into a sound sleep. I now propose to inject a stimulant which will end that sleep suddenly. When she wakes up, she will remember, I hope, that I have promised her perfect vision again. At the moment of her waking, I shall give her a happy shock through Mr Herron. I've discussed with him what he is to say in her hearing. It's my duty to explain my procedure to you, Doctor Landon, and to you, Doctor McKeever.'

Carew broke out: 'Wouldn't it have been *much* closer to regular procedure if you had consulted the doctors *before* you instituted this—this unusual treatment?'

'I was afraid,' said Kildare frankly, 'that they would object. They would not like my idea in promising her perfect vision, because if the experiment does not work, and if she does not have perfect sight when the bandages are removed, the shock may react detrimentally and confirm her hysteria.'

'Exactly,' said Landon. 'You're risking everything on this. It's neck or nothing.'

'It seemed to me,' said Kildare, 'that I had to devise the greatest possible happy expectation and then at the critical moment supply the greatest possible *happy* shock. I couldn't create the expectation without making the largest possible promise.'

'Irregular, dangerous, and highly dubious procedure throughout,' said Landon. 'McKeever, do you agree?'

McKeever, after a pause, said slowly: 'I'm afraid that I'm too old and conservative to agree with Doctor Kildare; and yet there's something in me that tells me he may be right. It's all or nothing.'

'But to make the promise—to risk everything!' groaned Carew.

Messenger said in a voice which extreme

tension made flat and mechanical: 'The case is entirely in your hands, Kildare. Whether you succeed or fail, you have my support.'

'If the experiment doesn't work, I accept the entire blame,' said Kildare, and went back to Nancy.

He gave the injection quickly, leaning over the bed, listened to her heart with a stethoscope. After a moment he said to Nora: 'She's waking up. Be here by the bed. Speak in a very quiet voice and say to her over and over: "Everything is all right, now!"'

'Everything is all right now, darling,' said Nora.

'Softer!'

'Everything is all right now, Nancy, dear,' murmured Nora.

'That's right. Keep saying that; and hold her hand. So.'

He went back into the next room. His face was white, but he had his jaw set, all the bulldog in him showing. He had left the connecting door open, and for a long moment the room was in silence, waiting. At length the voice of Nancy murmured something indistinguishable. They could barely hear the reassuring words of Nora as she said: 'It's all right, Nancy. My dear, it's all going to be right with you ...'

The voice of the girl came again more clearly.

'Now!' said Kildare, nodding to Herron,

and the big man made a gesture of assent. They faced the door of the sickroom together.

Kildare said loudly: 'She's in there, but she mustn't see you now.'

'I've *got* to see her,' said Herron.

'Keep your voice down,' commanded Kildare. 'These partitions are not very thick.'

'Whether she's blind forever or not, there's nobody in the world who means anything to me except Nancy!' said the booming voice of Herron.

'Charles! *Charles*!' cried Nancy from the next room.

'Go in—go in, you fool!' whispered Kildare. 'Push up the bandages . . .'

Herron, playing no role now, rushed into the room with great strides. Kildare closed the door except for an inch or two. He stared before him at the others, seeing nothing; then the girl's voice came to them high and sharp with an ecstasy of happiness: 'Charles, I *am* seeing you again. And you're not . . .'

Kildare shut the door fast behind him.

Paul Messenger spilled back in his chair suddenly on the verge of collapse. There was a confusion in the room; Carew was saying over and over again: 'He's done it! He's done it again!'

Kildare got hastily into the hall. Mary Lamont was waiting there.

'It's okay,' said Kildare. 'She's telling Herron how well she can see him. It's all over.'

He put his hands in his pockets and leaned his head and shoulders back against the wall.

'Funny how happy people can be, isn't it?' he asked.

'Yes, doctor,' said the girl.

'Stay around here. When the racketing dies down in there, you be on hand to reassure her. She's going to ask a thousand questions to find out how we discovered the truth. Tell her the facts—it was Gillespie who saw that it was plain hysteria. And he passed the hint along to me.'

'Gillespie? Did *he* do that?'

'He does everything around here. Everything that's worth while. So long, Mary.'

He had started down the hall when another thought struck him like a bullet and made his wince. 'Where's my father, Mary? I've got to get to him at once.'

'I've tried to tell you about him,' she said.

'You've never mentioned his name ... and he's ill. I've got to get straight to him.'

'I mentioned him. I tried to tell you that Doctor Gillespie has seen him.'

'Gillespie? Has he seen father? God bless him for that! What did he say?'

'It's nothing but old age. There's no heart trouble, Jimmy.'

'Say that again to me ... My God, Mary, I love you for saying that.'

There were at that moment in the hall nurses, two interns in the distance, a resident physician, and an orderly, but Kildare smashed a thousand rules as he leaned and kissed Mary Lamont.

'I hope this spoils your reputation, Mary,' he said. 'I hope I'm dragged up on the carpet to explain.'

She shook her head as she looked up at him.

'You'll never spoil any reputations,' she said. 'You're so—*damned* brotherly!... I think Doctor Gillespie would like to see you.'

'Like to see me?' repeated Kildare, astonished. He watched the tears coming into her eyes. 'What have you been up to?' he demanded.

'Nothing ... but he knows now why you stopped working with him.'

'He knows ... what?'

But without waiting for an answer, he turned and hurried down the hall. It was hours before the elevator came. It sank with monstrous leisure toward the lower floor. And the feet of Kildare could not get him quickly enough to the office of Gillespie. When he opened the door he found Molly Cavendish putting things in order.

'Do you think I could see the doctor?' asked Kildare, always a little overawed by her.

'I suppose that's your privilege ... if you care to use it,' said the Cavendish.

From the inside office the voice of Gillespie roared suddenly: 'Damn the rules! I want you to take your bloodhounds off the trail of that boy!'

The unmistakable voice of the chairman of the State Board of Health answered: 'Naturally, Leonard. Of course we will. But you must realize that young Kildare was very stubborn, refused to offer explanations, and we had no idea of the true nature of the case that involved him until you…'

'Run along! I'm busy!' bellowed Gillespie.

The chairman of the board 'ran along.' He exited so fast and in such a state of mental perturbation that he hardly glimpsed Kildare in the outer office. After a moment, Kildare tapped at the inner door and then opened it.

Gillespie, glancing up, made a furtive gesture with a cage of white mice which he had been holding in his lap. It was as though he were trying to hide it from the eyes of Kildare.

'No harm done, Jimmy,' he said. 'I was just *looking* at them. I wasn't going to *do* anything with them, doctor.'

He slipped the cage back into its proper place on the shelf. Kildare, amazed, could not speak a word.

Gillespie began to strike one calloused, dry hand into the other, frowning down at the floor.

'I suppose you're going to order me to get all these things out of my office—and out of my life, doctor?' asked Gillespie.

'I?—Order *you*?' exclaimed Kildare.

'After all,' said Gillespie, 'if I have to make a

choice, I suppose I'd a little rather have a Kildare than a room full of white mice . . . But I hate to see them go, doctor.'

Kildare made a slow gesture that indicated himself and Gillespie and the whole world.

'Don't you think that we might be able to go ahead with *everything*—but quietly?' he asked.

'I think what my physician permits me to think,' said Gillespie. 'I wonder if we *could* go on with it—very quietly, Jimmy, very quietly!'

Max Brand™ is the best-known pen name of Frederick Faust, creator of Dr Kildare,™ Destry, and many other fictional characters popular with readers and viewers worldwide. Faust wrote for a variety of audiences in many genres. His enormous output, totaling approximately thirty million words or the equivalent of 530 ordinary books, covered nearly every field: crime, fantasy, historical romance, espionage, Westerns, science fiction, adventure, animal stories, love, war, and fashionable society, big business and big medicine. Eighty motion pictures have been based on his work along with many radio and television programs. For good measure he also published four volumes of poetry. Perhaps no other author has reached more people in more different ways.

Born in Seattle in 1892, orphaned early, Faust grew up in the rural San Joaquin Valley of California. At Berkeley he became a student rebel and one-man literary movement, contributing prodigiously to all campus publications. Denied a degree because of unconventional conduct, he embarked on a series of adventures culminating in New York City where, after a period of near starvation, he received simultaneous recognition as a serious poet and successful popular-prose writer. Later, he traveled widely, making his home in

New York, then in Florence, and finally in Los Angeles.

Once the United States entered the Second World War, Faust abandoned his lucrative writing career and his work as a screenwriter to serve as a war correspondent with the infantry in Italy, despite his fifty-one years and a bad heart. He was killed during a night attack on a hilltop village held by the German army. New books based on magazine serials or unpublished manuscripts continue to appear. Alive and dead he has averaged a new one every four months for seventy-five years. In the U.S. alone nine publishers issue his work, plus many more in foreign countries. Yet, only recently have the full dimensions of this extraordinarily versatile and prolific writer come to be recognized and his stature as a protean literary figure in the 20th Century acknowledged. His popularity continues to grow throughout the world.

We hope you have enjoyed this Large Print book. Other Chivers Press or G.K. Hall Large Print books are available at your library or directly from the publishers. For more information about current and forthcoming titles, please call or write, without obligation, to:

Chivers Press Limited
Windsor Bridge Road
Bath BA2 3AX
England
Tel. (01225) 335336

OR

G.K. Hall
P.O. Box 159
Thorndike, Maine 04986
USA
Tel. (800) 223–2336

All our Large Print titles are designed for easy reading, and all our books are made to last.